"Unlike you, I do not lack experience."

"So I've gathered." Jacey's gaze slid to his, and he didn't trust the speculative gleam in her eyes. "Maybe you can help me, after all."

"Anything. As I've proven tonight, I'm at your service."

Jacey smiled, slow and satisfied, and he had the distinct sense that he'd stepped neatly into a trap. "That's just where I want you. At my service, so to speak."

Lucky choked. She couldn't possibly have meant that the way it had sounded. "Careful. A less astute man would have assumed you meant..."

"That I want to sleep with you? That *is* what I meant."

Lucky's throat seemed to have closed completely, his lungs shut down. But the rest of his body was showing remarkable signs of interest.

Dear Reader,

Welcome to the New Year—and to another month of fabulous reading. We've got a lineup of books you won't be able to resist, starting with the latest CAVANAUGH JUSTICE title from RITA® Award winner Marie Ferrarella. *Dangerous Disguise* takes an undercover hero, adds a tempting heroine, then mixes them up with a Mob money-laundering operation run out of a restaurant. It's a recipe for irresistibility.

Undercover Mistress is the latest STARRS OF THE WEST title from multi-RITA® Award-winning author Kathleen Creighton. A desperate rescue leads to an unlikely alliance between a soap opera actress who's nowhere near as ditsy as everyone assumes and a federal agent who's finally discovered he has a heart. In *Close to the Edge*, Kylie Brant takes a bayou-born private detective and his high-society boss, then forces them onto a case where "hands off" turns at last into "hands on." In Susan Vaughan's *Code Name: Fiancée,* when agent Vanessa Wade has to pose as the fiancée of wealthy Nick Markos, it's all for the sake of national security. Or is it? Desire writer Michelle Celmer joins the Intimate Moments roster with *Running on Empty*, an amnesia story that starts at the local discount store and ends up…in bed. Finally, Barbara Phinney makes her second appearance in the line with *Necessary Secrets*, introducing a pregnant heroine and a sexy cop— but everyone's got secrets to hide.

Enjoy them all, then come back next month for more of the best and most exciting romantic reading around.

Yours,

Leslie J. Wainger

Leslie J. Wainger
Executive Editor

Please address questions and book requests to:
Silhouette Reader Service
U.S.: 3010 Walden Ave., P.O. Box 1325, Buffalo, NY 14269
Canadian: P.O. Box 609, Fort Erie, Ont. L2A 5X3

Close to the Edge

KYLIE BRANT

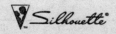

INTIMATE MOMENTS™

Published by Silhouette Books

America's Publisher of Contemporary Romance

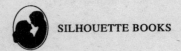 SILHOUETTE BOOKS

ISBN 0-373-27411-4

CLOSE TO THE EDGE

Visit Silhouette Books at www.eHarlequin.com

Printed in U.S.A.

Books by Kylie Brant

Silhouette Intimate Moments

McLain's Law #528
Rancher's Choice #552
An Irresistible Man #622
Guarding Raine #693
Bringing Benjy Home #735
Friday's Child #862
*Undercover Lover #882
*Heartbreak Ranch #910
*Falling Hard and Fast #959
Undercover Bride #1022
†Hard To Handle #1108
Born in Secret #1112

†Hard To Resist #1119
†Hard To Tame #1125
**Alias Smith and Jones #1169
**Entrapment #1221
**Truth or Lies #1238
**Dangerous Deception #1306
In Sight of the Enemy #1323
Close to the Edge #1341

*The Sullivan Brothers
†Charmed and Dangerous
**The Tremaine Tradition

KYLIE BRANT

lives with her husband and children. Besides being a writer, this mother of five works full-time teaching learning-disabled students. Much of her free time is spent in her role as professional spectator at her kids' sporting events.

An avid reader, Kylie enjoys stories of love, mystery and suspense—and she insists on happy endings. She claims she was inspired to write by all the wonderful authors she's read over the years. Now most weekends and all summer she can be found at the computer, spinning her own tales of romance and happily-ever-afters.

She invites readers to check out her online read in the reading room at eHarlequin.com. Readers can write to Kylie at P.O. Box 231, Charles City, IA 50616, or e-mail her at kyliebrant@hotmail.com. Her Web site is www.kyliebrant.com.

For Justin, the entertainer of the family.
I love you, sweetie!

Acknowledgment

Special thanks to Edward Fischer, forensic psychologist,
for your infinite patience with my questions about
private investigation. I value your assistance
and our conversations more than you can know!

Chapter 1

Lucky Boucher would have sworn that his day couldn't get any lousier. But it took an abrupt nosedive at about the same time the tony blonde walked into Frenchy's.

Not that he could totally blame the events of the day on the blonde. It wasn't her fault that his 1980 Firebird—on which he lavished as much time and devotion as a mother did on her infant—picked that morning to stage a most costly tantrum. Nor could he fault the woman for his hairstylist's distraction that afternoon, which had resulted in his hair being cut a full quarter-inch shorter than his specifications.

But from the moment she entered the place any thoughts he'd had of a relaxing evening were banished. He watched with a feeling of resignation as she swept the tavern's shabby interior with a regal gaze, then made her way toward the bar. There was a collective hiss, as if all the men in the place had simultaneously sucked in their guts and squared their shoulders.

With a mournful shake of his head, he returned his attention to his pool game. He wasn't one given to philosophizing, but there were a few absolutes in this world. Men would always act like fools when faced with a beautiful woman, even one as far out of their league as this one. And the presence of a classy female in a place like this was a powder keg waiting to detonate.

From the wisdom of experience he knew, as a rule, blondes were generally trouble.

However, he wasn't above using the diversion she posed to his own advantage. While his opponent was still drooling in her direction, Lucky sized up his shot, then banked the cue ball off one side of the table to kiss the three, sending it into the corner pocket.

The sound had his opponent, a thick muscle-bound man known only as Stally, swiveling his head back toward the table with a scowl on his face. "What the hell you doing?"

"Whippin' your ass in pool." Lucky straightened to chalk his cue stick, while considering his next play. "The fact that you have to ask makes me almost sorry about takin' your money." He sent the man an insincere grin. "Almost."

Stally's brows drew closer together. "Play don't continue 'til both players are looking at the table. That last shot of yours don't count."

Lucky leaned forward to line up his next shot, resting his cue lightly on his outstretched thumb to balance it. "What's that, some obscure rule from the pool etiquette handbook? Keep your attention on the game, *mon ami.* Perhaps you will learn something." The six was then sent spinning to a side pocket.

"He is generally an untrustworthy sort," Remy Delacroix, Lucky's supposed friend offered lazily from a nearby table. "You need to keep your eye on him at all times. Fortunately for you, I was watchin' the table. The shot was clean."

"I still don't like it."

With an inner sigh, Lucky deliberately botched his next attempt and stepped aside with a flourish. "I'll give you one last turn then. Make it count."

With a sneer, the man circled the table to study his options. Lucky used the time to check out the blonde's progress. The bar stool she'd chosen was right beside Goldie Bellow's, an all-around lowlife who made his living running girls through some of New Orleans' less savory hotels. Today the pimp was dressed in a lime-green suit with a bright-yellow shirt. Next to the woman's tailored white shirt and crisply pressed jeans, he looked like a gaudy plastic Mardi Gras bead set next to a pearl necklace.

While Lucky watched, the bartender put a drink before her and Bellows made a production of paying for it from a large roll of bills he'd taken from his pocket.

It hadn't escaped him that men were falling over themselves vacating nearby tables and filling the rest of the stools to get closer to the woman. He gave it another fifteen minutes before all hell broke loose.

Stally's muttered curse brought his gaze back to the pool table. The other man had managed to sink three balls before missing the fourth.

"Looks like you may have met your match, Boucher,"

Remy suggested, raising a finger to summon the waitress for another round.

"Your confidence is overwhelmin'. Watch and learn." Within short order, he sank his next three balls, and concentrated on dispatching the lone eight ball remaining. Raised voices from the direction of the bar had him mentally shaving five minutes off his original estimate. With unhurried motions, he lined up his last shot.

"Move over, buddy. It's my turn."

Stally's demand came just as Lucky was about to send the cue ball barreling into the eight. He lifted his head. "What are you babblin' about?"

With a threatening expression, the other man said, "You scratched. Just now. The tip of your stick touched the felt. I seen it plain as day." He glanced around at the other customers in the vicinity, as if looking for support. But it wasn't the swell of onlookers that had Lucky bending to his shot again. It was the sudden activity at the bar. Another man had made his move, and was trying to engage the blonde's attention.

"Right corner pocket." Lucky dispatched the last ball in short order, then straightened, his gaze on the woman, as he reached for the two fifties lying on the side of the table.

Stally's hand slapped down over his. "Like I said, you scratched. We'll play the game over."

"Why?" Lucky barely spared the man a glance. "Do you figure to play better the second time around?" Goldie was off his stool, he noted, one hand clamped around the blonde's arm. The other man was rising, as well, to lean menacingly across the woman. She looked like a very small, very defenseless rabbit trapped between two snarling wolves.

"You're a funny guy." Stally's voice lacked real appreciation. "But I said we'll play it over, so that's what we'll do. Unless you want everyone here to know that you're a coward, as well as a cheat."

"Um, if I may make an observation," Remy said diffidently, "he didn't scratch. Boucher doesn't cheat at pool. With women, yes. Can't be trusted around them. Wise men lock up their daughters when he's in the vicinity." There was a low murmur of agreement from the crowd that had gathered. "But pool...no. You got beat, my friend, fair and square."

"Thank you so much," Lucky told Remy with mock politeness. "Remind me to return the favor someday." He shifted his attention from his friend's grin to the man who still held his hand clapped over his. "It appears, *mon ami,* that no one agrees with you. So pay up, if you ever want to play here again."

It was long tension-filled seconds later before the man's grip loosened, and his hand was lifted away completely. "Wise choice." Lucky gave him a careless smile and scooped up the money, tucking it into his jeans pocket. His attention already diverted by the scene unfolding at the bar, he said, "Better luck next time."

"I'm not gonna forget this. What's your name—Bullshit?" Lucky stilled, re-focused on the man at his side. "Yeah, I ain't gonna forget you, Bullshit. This ain't over."

He barely heard Remy's groan. Didn't notice the sudden scrambling as men hastened to back away from the table. One moment the taller man was spitting on the floor between them, and the next moment Lucky was behind him, holding a cue stick across his throat, cutting off his oxygen.

"I am normally a very forgivin' kind of guy," Lucky said conversationally. Stally's hands were on the stick, trying to wrest it away, so he exerted more pressure on it. "You can call me a cheat. That is only your opinion, *n'est ce pas?* You can even call me a coward. After all, that's a matter of perception." An edge of steel entered his tone. "But you do not, ever, joke about my name. My *grand-mère* has always been a stickler about that. It's Boo-shin." He gave it the French pronunciation, with the final letter almost silent. The man gave a strangled gasp as a response. "Or if you can't manage that, Boo-shay is acceptable. Let me hear you try." He loosened the pressure slightly.

"Boo-shay," the man gasped, his voice hoarse.

Lucky freed him suddenly, his tone again amiable. "There, that was not so hard, was it?" Stally bent over, wheezing, and Lucky clapped him on the back. "I'm sure it was just a misunderstandin' on your part."

"You're crazy," the man sputtered, backing away even as he uttered the words.

Lucky's gaze went again to the bar, and he winced. Goldie and the stranger were trading punches, as the blonde was attempting to sidle out from between the two of them. With a crash, Goldie sent the other man into a table and jumped on him. The woman ducked to the floor. Ambling in the direction of the battle, he said, "At times like these, it is difficult to disagree with you."

Several patrons had surrounded the men, shouting encouragement and jeers. Money changed hands as bets on the outcome were made. The woman was easing toward the exit, but her escape was thwarted by a ponytailed biker who stood and grabbed her arm as she passed by. Lucky walked faster. Before he could reach the pair, she moved swiftly, ramming her knee into the man's groin, doubling him over. Then she sailed out the door.

Three other men began to follow her. Lucky beat them to the exit. "Goldie's offerin' a hundred to anyone who helps him out." Two of them stopped, turning to look speculatively at the couple on the floor. The third kept moving.

"She's not for the likes of you, friend." Lucky stiff-armed the man, preventing him from passing by. There was a loud crash as Goldie was tossed over the bar and into the bottles lined up in back of it. "It would be much healthier for you to watch the show in here."

"Hell with you, Boucher. You just want her for yourself."

It was easy enough to dodge the punch the man aimed at his stomach. But as the crowd shifted, pressing in closer to the battle near the bar, Lucky was thrown off balance. He didn't quite manage to duck the left jab the man threw. It snapped his head back, and for a moment he saw stars. The man pushed by him, then tripped over Lucky's outstretched leg. A well-aimed push had him flat on his face, and in the next moment Lucky's knee was in his back. Taking the man's head between his hands, Lucky rapped it smartly against the floor, felt the guy go limp. Giving it another rap for good measure, he rose, wiggled his jaw gingerly.

"Looks like you're goin' to have a bruise, my friend." Lucky sent a disparaging glance at Remy, who looked as though he was enjoying himself hugely. "As always, your assistance is greatly appreciated."

"I had your back," Remy assured him, tipping the bottle of beer to his lips. With a meaningful glance toward the door, he noted, "You know, that blonde isn't your type either."

Lucky pushed out of the bar, his friend's words echoing in his ears. High-class former debutantes were about as far from his usual female companions as it was possible to be. He liked to believe, however, that it was by choice. *His.*

When he hit the sidewalk he became aware that a slight mist was falling. Perfect. Hunching his shoulders, he jammed his hands in the pockets of his jeans and headed down the street. Given the events of the evening, he didn't need any further proof of his earlier conviction. Blondes were trouble. Always.

Keeping an eye on the clock on her office wall, Jacinda Eloise Wheeler unbuttoned her plain white shirt with one hand and undid her jeans with the other. Shimmying out of the denim, she stripped off her socks and leaned against the corner of her desk to draw first one, then the other thigh-high nylon over her legs. With any luck she could slip into the Sisters of the South Auxillary gathering before dinner was served. That timing, she hoped, would save her from her mother's inevitable disapproval.

There was a tiny noise behind her. Whirling, she saw her office door swing open, a dark shape of a man filling it. A strangled scream escaped her throat, even as she reached behind her, searching her desktop for a weapon. Her fingers closed around a heavy paperweight just as the figure stepped into the room.

Then her eyelids slid closed in relief. "Damn you, Boucher, you scared me to death."

Lucky's face was lit with unmistakable male appreciation. "If you had shown just a little bit of those riches back at the bar, *cher*, your evenin' might have been a bit more productive."

For a moment she stared at him blankly, before following his gaze to her chest. She dropped the paperweight and yanked her shirt closed, felt her cheeks firing. "A gentleman," she pointed out from between clenched teeth, "wouldn't have looked."

"What have I ever done to give you the impression that I'm a gentleman?"

He managed, she thought, to sound affronted. And he was right. Of all the descriptives she could come up with, *gentleman* would never make the list. He looked more like one of Lucifer's henchmen, handpicked to roam the earth wreaking havoc on the female population. The light rain had dampened his black hair, which was always kept just a shade too long. Right now it nearly touched his collar in the back, though he'd claimed he was leaving early to get a haircut that afternoon. Given his aversion to shaving, his jaw was most often shadowed. They'd long ago reached a compromise so that he used a razor at least every other day, making him due again tomorrow. His eyes, as dark as his hair, usually held a wicked gleam that, if rumors could be believed, had led hundreds of unwary female hearts to their ruination.

The lazy bayou cadence of his languid drawl put

most people at ease, but the more wary would never mistake him for harmless. Not with that slight hint of menace layered beneath the lazy affability. Given his penchant for jeans and T-shirts emblazoned with suggestive sayings, he looked like exactly what he was—a man who had grown up in the swamps and had lived by his wits in the back alleys of New Orleans. The fresh bruise blooming below one eye only added to his aura of danger.

He ambled into the room and propped his hips against a chair to survey her. "What were you doin' in Frenchy's tonight?"

"I am not going to stand here half naked and have a conversation with you!"

His mouth twitched. "A shame, since you make such a picture half naked." When she reached for the paperweight again, he made a production of raising his hands and turned his back with exaggerated care. "What could you possibly be plannin' after startin' a riot in Frenchy's? Wrestlin' a few alligators? Leapin' tall buildings with a single bound?"

"I'm meeting my mother for dinner." And, she realized, with another quick glance at the clock, she was almost certain to be late. Giving up the battle, she slipped the shirt off and let it fall to the floor. "Hand me that dress, will you?"

He reached for the sedate black dress hanging over the back of the chair and held it up to study it. "A present from a nun?"

She snatched it from him, yanked down the zipper, and stepped into it. "From my mother."

"That explains it. But it doesn't answer my question."

Struggling to zip up, she said, "I got a tip this afternoon about that missing girl, Cheryl Kenning. Remember her?"

"Twenty-year-old, reported missin' by her grandparents. The NOPD found her hookin', didn't they?"

"That's the one." She jammed her feet into her high-heeled pumps. "I discovered that she was working for Goldie, and with a little digging I was able to come up with a list of his hangouts."

Without asking permission, he spun around to frown at her. "And you thought you'd just ask him to point you in her general direction?"

"Give me some credit. I heard he carried his business ledger with him." She rounded the desk to pull open the center drawer. Withdrawing a small black notebook, she waggled it, feeling smug. "This fell on the floor after I arranged to have him distracted. I managed to swipe it on my way out."

"You arranged? The guy that provoked him was workin' with you?"

One of the nice things about Lucky, she thought, as she dropped the notebook back in the drawer, was that he caught on so quickly. She never had to waste time explaining things.

Admiration sounded in his voice. "Very nice. Devious, yet simple."

"Thank you. I learned from the master." She went to her bag, withdrew a small purse that would match the dress, and began transferring a few things from the one she'd carried earlier. "Apparently each girl he has working for him frequents the same few locations. I'll spend some time staking them out, and then when I can be cer-

tain of the location Cheryl frequents, I'll let her grandparents know."

"So they can do what? Kidnap her?"

Snapping her purse closed, she searched the bag for
the flat jewelry box that held her grandmother's pearls.
Pushing aside a tiny sliver of uncertainty, she responded,
"That will be up to them. My job was just to find her.
Help me with these, will you?"

Lucky moved in back of her and took the two ends
of the necklace and fastened the clasp. But when he was
done, he didn't step away. He turned her around, his
hands remaining on her arms, his face serious. "She
had a chance to leave that life the last time the police
picked her up, and her grandparents were alerted.
Maybe she doesn't want to leave, have you ever thought
of that? You may not approve of her choice, but she still
has the right to make it."

It wasn't the first time they'd disagreed over a case.
It wouldn't be the last. Their backgrounds couldn't be
more different, and the difference was inevitably reflected in their attitudes. But knowing that, understanding it, didn't make it any less annoying this time. "My
approval doesn't have anything to do with it. He might
have gotten her hooked on drugs. Or she might be too
afraid of him to leave. She'll get her choice, and it won't
be tempered by fear or addiction."

Not every case handled by Wheeler and Associates
was imbued with moral implications. Most, as a matter
of fact, bordered on the mundane. But there were cases,
plural, and the knowledge filled Jacey with a quiet sense
of satisfaction. She'd started the private investigation
business as soon as she could get her hands on her trust-

fund monies, over the vehement objections of her mother. She'd acquired the training, found the building and done the advertising. And then, for the better part of a year, she'd twiddled her thumbs.

It seemed that few in her circle of acquaintances had need for a PI, however upscale and discreet. And most who had stopped in had lost interest quickly when it became apparent that hers was a one-woman operation. That had abruptly changed when Lucky Boucher had walked through her door three years ago.

Rather than bringing her a case, he'd been looking for work. The idea had been laughable, since she couldn't even keep herself busy. And he…he had been completely inappropriate, even if she had been considering employees. He was too rough, too unpolished and his background bordered on the unsavory. He'd also been impossible to get rid of.

He'd snatched the lone case file off her desk and read it over her furious objection. Then he'd left, after vowing to find the bail jumper she'd been hired to trace within twenty-four hours.

It had taken him six.

After two weeks and two more solved cases, his constant badgering had worn her down. Besides, as he'd pointed out then, he worked cheap. She'd hired him reluctantly, fully expecting him to tire of the job and move on within weeks. He'd surprised them both by staying. Even more shocking, they had somehow, along the way, become friends.

At least, she thought that was what they were. She trusted him, in a way she did no other, although at times it was difficult to tell just who was the boss and who was the employee. She seemed to spend most of her time re-minding him.

He dropped his hands, freeing her. But instead of moving away, she frowned, reached up to touch the fresh bruise on his face. "Did your pool partner catch up with you after I left?"

He'd never been one to miss a chance to milk an opportunity. Making a show of wincing, he said, "No, this *bouele* was delivered by one of your would-be admirers. There were several who thought of followin' you out of the bar. I convinced them otherwise."

Rather than looking grateful, she appeared mildly amused. "So you were protecting me? Lucky, that's so sweet."

Discomfited, he shrugged. There was something about the woman that could make him feel like a tongue-tied twelve-year-old. He didn't much care for the sensation. "Well, if one had hurt you, I'd have had to do all the work around here. Since I already carry more than my load, I was just thinkin' of myself."

She made a sound that almost qualified as a sniff, one she often used to denote derision and disagreement without having to do something as ill-bred as argue. It never failed to set his teeth on edge.

"I think I demonstrated my ability to take care of myself in there. Was that biker walking again by the time you left?"

He hadn't been, but Lucky didn't want to swell her head by telling her so. "Next time give him a good kick once he's down. You want to disable him completely, not just piss him off."

"Thank you so much." From the sweet smile she

was gracing him with, he was given the impression that she was considering carrying out his advice on him. "But I don't have time for your lavish compliments." She glanced at the clock and made a face, reaching for a ridiculously small purse. "I should have called for a cab, but it's too late. And my mother is going to be impossible."

"That goes without sayin'." *Impossible* was a much more favorable description than any he would have come up with. He and Charlotte Marie Pembrooke Wheeler regarded each other with thinly veiled contempt.

"All right." She gave a deep breath, smoothed her hair. "How do I look?"

With a critical eye, he surveyed her. "Prim as a librarian. A very dull librarian."

"Why would I even ask you?" she muttered, opening her purse and taking out her lipstick. Crossing to a mirror on the opposite wall, she applied it carefully. "You've made your preferences regarding women's attire all too clear."

He slouched against the wall to watch her. "Low-cut top, short skirt, panties optional. Choices that never go out of fashion."

"Any question about your fashion sense is answered by reading the shirts you insist on wearing."

Offended, he looked down at his favorite black T-shirt, which proclaimed I love everybody. You're next. "You're just bein' mean because you have to spend the evenin' with your mother."

She blotted her lipstick and dropped the tissue in the wastebasket. "I have to go. Lock up for me, will you? And don't forget to set the alarm. And check the windows. And make sure the door closes tightly behind you. It kind of sticks, you know, and I'm afraid…"

He gave her a friendly nudge out the office door. "I know how to lock up. Go. Have as good a time as possible with the Witches of the South."

He thought, he was almost certain, he heard a smile in her voice. "Sisters of the South. Thanks. And you get one of your girlfriends to look at that bruise. I'm sure, given your skills, you can appear pathetic enough to be plied with TLC all night."

The thought was cheering. "If not, I'm losin' my touch." And there was no reason, none at all, to believe that was true. He stood watching while she dashed through the rain to the car she'd parked right in front of the business. It wasn't until the taillights winked and she pulled away, that he turned back to the office, already flipping through a mental file. Who should he call? Desiree? Leanne? Monique? Reaching for the phone, he punched in a number. With a pitying look at the now-empty street, Lucky was certain of one thing. Whatever he ended up doing this evening, it would beat what Jacey had waiting for her, hands down.

Chapter 2

"I've made your apologies to the hostess."

The first words Charlotte Wheeler spoke were delivered in her customary genteel voice, carefully modulated. But years of experience had Jacey reading the disapproval layered beneath. *Your late arrival is insufferably rude. There is no reason, short of death, that could possibly excuse your tardiness.*

And because no excuse would mollify her mother, least of all the truth, Jacey didn't offer any. "Thank you. Have you found your table setting yet?"

Charlotte's lips tightened just a fraction. "We're seated together. I waited for you before dining. I didn't want to disturb the others at our table by both of us holding up their meals."

Years of practice had her skirting the verbal land

mine. "Let's sit then, shall we? You're looking lovely to-night. I always like that color on you."

That, at least, could be said honestly. Charlotte's dress was the same bottle-green color as her eyes. She was sixty, and, thanks to a skilled and discreet plastic surgeon, looked fifteen years younger. Her brown hair was worn short, as Charlotte subscribed to the outdated belief that a woman of a certain age should never wear long hair. It wasn't the only antiquated notion she clung to, nor the only one they disagreed upon.

Jacey followed her mother across the crowded room, stopping several times to return greetings and exchange pleasantries. The contrast between the staid dinner and the smoky bar she'd left less than an hour ago couldn't be more stark. If her mother had her way, Jacey's entire adult life would be filled with more of the same; an endless parade of boring functions, peopled by equally dull members of what passed for New Orleans' high society.

A shudder worked down her spine at the thought. They were shown to their table by a white-jacketed waiter who seated them, then summoned another to bring their plates. Every time Jacey wearied of the constant battles with her mother over her choice of careers, she had only to think of events like this to feel her resolve stiffen. That strength was necessary. Battles with Charlotte Marie Pembrooke Wheeler could leave lasting wounds.

The upside of her tardiness was that she was still eating when the guest speaker was introduced, which gave her something to focus on besides what promised to be an excruciatingly long-winded speech. With an ease born of long practice, Jacey assumed a politely inter-ested expression and tuned the woman out.

It wasn't that she didn't care about the plight of the walruses, which was the current issue of the moment for the Sisters of the South Auxillary. Jacey would be happy to write a check, which was the pitch the speaker was working up to. But it seemed like the venues selected for the fund-raisers—fancy dinners or formal balls— were a bit ironic. Why not spend the money instead on the cause itself, and eliminate one layer of cost?

Her mind drifted to her business. She needed more help. Not that there had been any truth to Lucky's breezy assertion that he carried more than his share of the weight, but there was no denying that a third investiga-tor would lighten the load for them both. It was a nice problem to have, especially since there had been a time a few years ago when she'd almost despaired of getting to this point. But her business had been self-supporting for two years now. She no longer had to dip into her trust fund to pay her bills. Joan, her secretary, had her hands full managing the office, but Jacey didn't think they were yet at the place where they could keep another full-timer busy. She decided to advertise next week for part-time help, and have the new employee handle some of the research.

Twenty minutes later there was a burst of applause and Jacey joined in, already calculating how much longer she'd have to stay. She'd be required to mingle, of course. Her mother would insist on that. But with any luck she could fulfill her obligations and be home in an hour.

The thought of her comfortable home in the French Quarter beckoned. Once she got there she'd chase away the chill from the evening rain by wrapping up on her couch in a quilt, with a hot drink and maybe an ice pack for her knee. It still throbbed, just a bit from the blow she'd landed on the biker. She could only hope that he was nursing a far more serious injury.

She parted from her mother, making the rounds as quickly as she could manage. Jacey had just stopped to speak to Suzanne Shrever, a former classmate of hers, when she felt eyes on her. She turned around, scanning the crowd, but saw nothing out of the ordinary.

"Honestly, Jacinda," Suzanne was saying, "I'm so envious of you with your exciting career. Is it very dangerous?"

That question was difficult to answer, Jacey thought, knowing that Suzanne's idea of danger was hiring a new caterer.

"I'm careful," she said, "and most of my work is routine. Missing persons, serving summonses, theft detection." She was careful to remain vague. Although most of her cases were just that unexceptional, all she needed was for her mother to get wind of details such as her experience earlier today. She'd learned long ago that skirmishes with Charlotte were safer when she didn't provide her with ammunition.

"Well," Suzanne tossed her artfully styled curls, "I just think you're the bravest thing. Bitsy didn't think you'd show up here tonight, but I said that very thing, I said, well of course she will, Jacinda is just so brave." She nodded vigorously.

The sensation was back, as if eyes were boring into her. "Well, that's nice," Jacey said inanely, scanning the crowd over the other woman's shoulder. She found the source of the feeling standing across the room at the balcony doors. The man was instantly recognizable, with his mane of silver hair and neat mustache. J. Walter Garvey, a local shipping magnate, gave her a nod when their gazes met and then, with a slight inclination of his head toward the doors, he went outside.

Suzanne's voice bubbled around her, but it might as well have been the drone of bees. Jacey looked around, trying and failing to see anyone else that the man might have been gesturing to. Curiosity, the bane of her existence, surged. More than half convinced she was going to make a fool of herself, she excused herself from her friend and made her way toward the half-open balcony door.

She found the older man leaning against the railing, smoking a thin cigar. The rain had stopped, but the early-fall air was still heavy with moisture. Jacey stepped outside and then hesitated, once again questioning her action. The Garvey family was reputed to be among the wealthiest in the city, due in no small part to the solitary man on the balcony. And although she knew him to speak to, having met him at various functions much like this one, she could think of no reason for him to seek her out.

"Close the door behind you and come here." The man's voice sounded a trifle testy. "There's no telling how long I can dodge that throng inside. There's always a few who'll use an event like this one to try to hit me up about a new business venture."

Jacey strolled over to his side, immediately wishing for a coat. She hadn't thought to bring a wrap when she'd tossed some things into the car to change into after work. "Mr. Garvey." She joined him at the railing, felt her skin dewed by the thick moisture in the air. "How have you been?"

"Not worth a damn."

She smiled a little. She'd always appreciated his tendency to speak his mind. Her smile faded when, in the next instant he added, "I'm dying."

Her face jerked to his, saw the truth of his words written there. "I'm sorry." The words were simple, heartfelt.

He waved them away. "Cancer. Nothing to be done about it, and I'd appreciate you keeping this to yourself. Haven't even told my family. I never could stand people blathering over me."

No, pity wouldn't be something this man would suffer easily. Even knowing as little as she did about him, Jacey recognized that. Rather than giving him any, she matched his matter-of-fact tone with one of her own. "What can I do?"

"I'm looking for someone to conduct research for me. I've considered several local investigative agencies, but think you might be better suited than most to fill this assignment."

A quiet hum of pleasure filled her at his words, followed by a leap of interest. This was what she needed, this constant challenge of matching her wits to solve puzzles, work out problems. She liked to think she was good at it, too. "I'm glad to hear that."

In the next moment he slipped out of his suit jacket and draped it around her shoulders. The old-fashioned courtliness of the gesture was at odds with his reputation for ruthlessness, both in business and with his family. "I've built Garvey Enterprises into a heavily diversified global operation. Started at a time when the business was more like bare-knuckled fighting than end-less bickering in corporate boardrooms." From his tone, it was easy to tell he much preferred the former. "I can't take it with me when I die, and I don't mind telling you, that fact irritates the hell out of me."

She smiled, surveying him in the dim spill of light afforded through the closed balcony doors. "Who will step into your shoes when you're gone?"

He gave a short nod of approval, drew on his cigar again. "You've cut to the heart of the matter. I'd heard you were quick. The fact is, Miss Wheeler, I don't know the answer to that question. That's where you come in."

Brows skimming upward, she asked, "You want me to tell you who to leave your business to?"

"Few men are fortunate in both business and family. Or maybe I just failed with mine." He gave a shrug that seemed more impatient than regretful. "My children were overindulged when they were young, and they haven't improved with age. Rupert, my son, is a skirt-chasing spendthrift, and my daughter, Lianna, is a pea-brained socialite with the morals of an alley cat. Their offspring don't look any more promising, but they're all I've got to work with. I need you to find out more about them, their strengths, if they have any, as well as any weaknesses. If there's one in the lot who's worthy, there will still be a Garvey at the helm of the business, at least for another generation. If I decide, based on the infor-mation you find for me, that they're all as useless as their parents..." He inhaled, then blew a perfect smoke ring. "Well, then the business will be completely incorpo-rated, with each of the family members getting a small share, and no real power in the way it's run."

She studied the man, fascinated by the scene he'd detailed for her. "It must be difficult to contemplate your company in the hands of strangers."

"Not as difficult as thinking of it in the hands of an incompetent, family or not."

Jacey could appreciate the sentiment. Wheeler and Associates had been her brainchild. She'd been the one with the dream, the ambition, and the guts to see her vision come to life. She'd close the doors before she'd see it run improperly. "So you want me to look into the backgrounds of your grandchildren, then let you know what I find out."

"That, and I want your personal observations on each." Catching her look of surprise, he tapped his cigar on the railing to remove the ash, and then continued. "Any firm could get me the information I need, but you…you travel in the same circles. With your social connections, there isn't a party or snooty affair you couldn't get an invitation to, and that, my dear, is why I chose you. I've always thought if you really want to see what makes a person tick, observe them in a social arena like the one inside." With a jerk of his head, he indicated the gathering on the other side of the doors. "Over time, everyone shows their true colors, and whether you love that type of thing or hate it as much as I do, these events can be a mine of information."

The words cast a decided pall over her earlier enthusiasm. Glancing through the double doors, she gave an inner sigh. He was right, and she would have arrived at the same conclusion eventually. A good PI used every avenue at her disposal. It was surely a flaw in her genetic makeup that she would have preferred more nights like the one she'd spent in Frenchy's than time spent at functions just like this one.

"What do you say, Miss Wheeler? Do you want the case?"

Without a hint of hesitation she answered, "Absolutely."

"Good." His tone suggested that he'd expected no other answer. He took her hand, pumped it hard twice before releasing it. "I'll send over a file in the morning that will give you the basic data on each of my grandchildren, as well as my contact information. I'll want regular updates."

She nodded. "I'll fill you in weekly. Would you like to come in to sign the contract, or should I have it delivered to you?"

"Deliver it to Garvey headquarters. The less we're seen together the better chance we have of keeping our association under wraps."

Now that he'd enlisted her cooperation, he appeared eager to be alone again. Jacey let the suit jacket slide off her shoulders and handed it to him. "I'll talk to you soon," she promised, and turned to walk toward the doors. Before entering the ballroom again, she took one last look at the man who'd just hired her.

Garvey was leaning heavily against the railing, the cigar in one hand, his jacket in the other. There was an aura of loneliness about his figure, one he would have been the first to deny. She felt a flicker of sympathy. Despite his family, the man was destined to die the same way he'd hacked out a niche in the corporate world. Alone.

Once inside, she looked for her mother to say her goodbyes and make her escape. But once she found her, Charlotte dashed Jacey's hopes of salvaging a portion of the evening with a quiet hour or two at home before bed.

"Did you hire a limo or drive yourself?"

"I drove," she said automatically, then immediately wished the words back. That would probably be enough to set her mother off on a disapproving lecture about maintaining appearances.

But this time Charlotte surprised her. "Wonderful, then you can give me a ride home. After John dropped me here, I gave him the rest of the night off."

Jacey blinked in surprise. Her mother wasn't exactly known for her largesse with employees. "I could call for a taxi if you want."

"That won't be necessary. I'm right on your way."

She was at least twenty minutes in the other direction, but Jacey pressed her lips together and did a mental count to ten. She could hardly refuse without seeming churlish, and making it appear that she didn't want to spend any more time than possible in her mother's presence.

Just because that fact happened to be true, didn't make it any less discourteous.

Silently kissing away the fantasy she'd had of spending a couple of hours unwinding, she accompanied her mother in search of their hostess. Her temples began to throb. There wasn't a doubt in her mind that the headache would only worsen before the evening was over.

The gates to the huge estate swung open slowly, and Jacey nosed her car up the long circular drive. Darkness had fallen over the meticulous lawn and ornamental shrubbery. She had always thought the home looked best in the dark. With the windows lit from within, the mansion took on a deceptively warm and inviting air. In the daylight, its uncompromising lines and precise land-scaping made it seem much more rigid, impersonal.

Much like its lone occupant.

"Just leave your car in front. I'll have cook serve us tea in the drawing room." As Jacey pulled to a stop, Charlotte's hand went to the door handle.

"I really can't come in, Mother. It's been a long day and I have an early start tomorrow. But I'll call you tomorrow night, I promise."

"Don't be ridiculous." With her usual tactics, Charlotte steamrollered over Jacey's excuses. "We have to discuss this situation you're in, and I refuse to do that over the phone."

Situation? Jacey rubbed her temples as her mother got out of the car. The hammering within was taking on a life of its own. Had Charlotte overheard Garvey? Or had she somehow caught wind of what had occurred at Frenchy's? She rejected both notions, even as she turned off the ignition and got out of the car. It would be just like her mother to be talking about her "little hobby," as she liked to call Wheeler and Associates. She had a feeling that the upcoming conversation was one they'd had many times before, and there was no new ground to be covered.

Nevertheless, she followed her mother up the orna-mental brick walk, and into the house. With her sore knee and headache, she was feeling just bitchy enough to be more blunt than usual when she told her mother to butt out. Again.

Charlotte was already replacing the receiver to the house phone in its cradle when Jacey stepped into the graceful drawing room. Like its owner, it was carefully accessorized to reflect elegance and good taste. With its paintings and objects of art it always reminded Jacey of a museum. Beautiful, but curiously lifeless.

"Well, this latest situation you're embroiled in is embarrassing, to say the least. However, I have thought of a way for you to salvage a bit of dignity from the mess." Charlotte heaved a sigh, and set her purse on the walnut credenza.

"Why don't you let me decide what's right for me, Mother? I've been an adult for some time now."

She might as well not have spoken. Charlotte was continuing. "It's not totally your fault, of course. I must say, I never expected Peter to behave so badly. But he is a man, after all, and you can be assured that people will be more forgiving of his boorishness than they would be of a woman's." She sat on the Louis XXIV armchair, and waved Jacey to the nearby matching settee.

She remained standing, attempting to make sense of her mother's words. "Peter? *My* Peter? Why? What has he done?"

Charlotte looked coolly amused for a moment. "Well, he's hardly yours anymore, now is he?"

The conversation was taking on the complication of a maze. "No, that is, we're on a break, but…" Jacey shook the unusual muzziness from her brain and demanded, "Why don't you just tell me what you're talking about? What is this about Peter Brummond?"

As an answer Charlotte rose, went to the French provincial desk in the corner of the room and returned with a cream-colored envelope, which she handed to her daughter. With impatience mounting, Jacey opened the flap to withdraw a heavily embossed invitation and scanned it quickly. Then she stopped, stared harder at the note in her hand, and sat down heavily on the settee.

You are cordially invited to an engagement party for
Peter Alexander Brummond
and
Celeste Emilie Longwaite, to be held...

"Good heavens, you really didn't know? Don't tell me he compounded his gauche behavior by not even inviting you?"

She tried to swallow, found her throat too dry. She had a mental flash of a very similar envelope lying, still unopened on her hallway table, with a pile of other correspondence she hadn't gotten around to yet.

"No. I mean, yes, I received one, but I've been so busy…" Her voice trailed off as she continued to gaze at the invitation, as if she could make sense of it through sheer force of will. Peter was getting married. To someone else.

"You really have to open your mail promptly, Jacinda." Exasperation sounded in her mother's voice. "I'm surprised someone at the Auxilliary tonight didn't mention this to you, and just think how difficult that would have been."

Difficult. A wild laugh welled up in Jacey's throat. She only barely managed to restrain it. Yes, she supposed it would have been difficult to hear from an acquaintance that the man she'd parted from three months ago in a mutual agreement to—"take a break for a bit and see where we're at"—had, in that time, met someone else and proposed marriage to her. A proposal he hadn't tendered to Jacey during their eighteen months together.

Not that she'd wanted him to. But still.

"I think Suzanne might have been referring to it to-night, but I wasn't really paying attention," she mur-mured, the invitation clutched tightly in her fingers. She raised her gaze to meet her mother's, nearly flinched. There was a sort of impatient pity in the woman's eyes that was somehow harder to face than the usual biting disapproval.

"Suzanne Shrever is an addlepated gossip. But I'm sure she's not saying anything that isn't being repeated ad nauseum in our circle." An expression of distaste crossed her face. There was little Charlotte Wheeler ab-horred more than being the target of gossip. "Damage control is of paramount importance at this point."

"Damage control." A blessed sort of numbness had settled over Jacey. "This isn't a military operation, Mother." She had a brief mental flash of Charlotte in uni-form, stars on her shoulders, helmet and jack boots. She wasn't so certain the woman hadn't missed her calling.

"Reputations are fragile things, Jacinda. I've let it be known, quietly of course, that you've been seeing some-one from out of town. We'll have to act quickly so that you can line up an escort in time for the party. Had you answered any of my phone messages for the last week, we could have already gotten started on this."

The words seemed to come from a distance. Anger burned through Jacey's numbness. How dare Peter do this to her! The emotion was welcome, and she seized on it gratefully. It was easier to focus on than to ac-knowledge the rest of the tangled feelings crashing through her. Humiliation. Shock. Hurt.

A glance at her mother's face had her shoving all that

aside for the moment. She needed every wit about her in order to deal with Charlotte. "That won't be necessary. I'm not going."

"Of course you'll go." The certainty in her tone had Jacey's jaw tightening. "Your failure to appear will only set people to talking even more. I'll have Dorothy Genesson tell her bridge group that you'll be bringing the new man in your life. She'll hint about the seriousness of your relationship, and then we'll let the word get around. You won't have to stay long, but to save face you do have to attend, and appear madly happy with your current companion."

Dorothy Genesson was as close to a best friend as Charlotte had. Both of them had been widowed for nearly ten years, and neither were eager to change that status. "Very Machiavellian, Mother. But there is no new man in my life." Not that she had missed the lack overmuch in the last few months. "And I tend to think that beating the bushes for a man to playact with at the engagement party is even more pathetic than showing up alone, or not at all."

"You always put the most negative spin on things. One does what the situation calls for."

Just for a moment, Jacey thought of the biker she'd dropped earlier that evening. Somehow she didn't think Charlotte would appreciate the association. "That's always been my philosophy."

"Excellent." Her mother crossed to her and handed her a paper with a list of names printed neatly on it. Each was followed by an address and phone number. She must have taken it from the desk when she'd retrieved the invitation. "Dorothy and I put our heads together and came up with this list of five men. Each lives out of town, is single and would be a suitable escort. I assumed you'd like to do the contact and final selection yourself."

The sheer gall of the action left Jacey speechless for a moment. Incredulity shredded that reaction, though, and quickly. "You've got to be joking. You expect me to call up some total strangers and beg for a date to my ex-boyfriend's engagement party? This sounds like the plot for a very bad chick-flick."

"Don't be irreverent." Charlotte sat down again. "You needn't pursue a relationship with the man you decide upon, although any of the five would be quite appropriate, if you should decide to do so."

"I'll bet." Cynicism flickered. She imagined that her mother had examined the bloodlines and portfolios of each and every candidate before placing his name on the list. "If I remember correctly, you approved of Peter, too, until quite recently."

Voice sharpening, Charlotte said, "I won't tolerate your impudence, Jacinda. Peter Brummond would have made an excellent match, and you have only yourself to blame for this fiasco."

Settling back against the uncomfortable settee, Jacey readied for battle. This, then, was the crux of the conversation. Not the faux sympathy, nor the matter-of-fact plotting. If truth be known, she had far more experience dealing with her mother's censure than with her understanding. "How exactly is that, Mother? Should I have had him shackled after we broke up so that he couldn't meet anyone else?" She pretended to consider the idea. "Possible, perhaps, but leg irons are so difficult to come by."

"If you had played your cards right, you could have finessed a proposal from him and this invitation would have your name on it, instead of that of some little social climber from Baton Rouge. You certainly had the time."

"Finessed a proposal." To give her hands something to do, she smoothed her dress over her legs. "That sounds very romantic."

"You know what I mean. Romance is vastly over-rated in these situations, at any rate. What matters most are similar backgrounds, breeding and position."

She'd heard her mother's views on marriage often enough to repeat them verbatim. They saddened and ter-rified her by turn. "If Peter and I had been interested in marriage, don't you think it would have come up over the course of eighteen months?"

"If he wasn't interested, you can blame that hobby of yours. What man wants to be married to a woman who insists on dealing with the criminal element all day long, and most weekends, as well?"

She opened her mouth, intending to straighten her mother out about her job again, then closed it. It was useless, and it really wasn't the issue here.

Charlotte went on. "I just don't understand you any-more, Jacinda. You never used to be so difficult. You were always such a pliable girl."

Weak, Jacey silently interpreted. Scared of her moth-er's displeasure, which could be earned so easily. Anx-ious to do whatever it took to please her, until she found that by doing so she was very rarely pleasing herself. It was shaming to admit, even to herself, just how much courage it had taken to stand up to Charlotte about her choice of careers. A lifetime of choosing the path of least resistance, she'd found, hadn't prepared her for the task.

However, constant practice was making it easier.

The jackhammering in her temples made it difficult to concentrate. She rose. There was nothing left to say, at any point. "I have to leave, Mother. I...appreciate the worry you've gone through. But don't concern yourself. I'll take care of it."

She began to cross to the door. Charlotte stood as well, just as the cook, Luella, entered with a tray of tea. "Don't go yet. We need to develop a plan of action."

"No, *we* don't need to do anything. This is my problem, and I'll take care of it in my own way." Taking advantage of her mother's unwillingness to discuss anything personal in front of the servants, Jacey continued with her escape. "I'll call you in a couple of days, all right?"

There was no mistaking the disapproval in Charlotte's silence, but Jacey was far past a time when it could change her mind. Slipping out the heavy front door, she hurried down the steps and to the car, a familiar sense of relief nearly swamping her.

Those who turn and run away live to fight another day. Her father's oft-repeated saying sounded in her mind. It had always been accompanied with a conspiratorial wink. He hadn't been one to confront his wife on many matters, opting instead for peaceful co-existence.

The rain had grown heavier. The streetlights shot the wet pavement with tiny splinters of light. She drove slowly, her headlights barely denting the inky darkness. Her earlier relief began to dissipate as the full weight of the situation struck her.

She supposed, by her mother's definition, she and Peter had been perfectly matched. With his tall blond good looks, they'd made, Charlotte had often said, a handsome couple. Certainly he'd come from a family whose background and fortune had been deemed appropriate by her mother, as well. Jacey had known him since she was a child, and she'd wondered, the last several months of their relationship, if that long acquaintance was to blame for the lack of any real... passion between them. They'd seemed more like a couple married twenty years than two people supposedly in love.

She didn't even remember now which of them had first proposed the idea of stepping back from the relationship for a while. It had been Peter, she was almost certain of it, but she'd seized on the idea with an eagerness that had been just as telling. And there was no use being less than honest, nothing she'd experienced during their time apart had made her regret the decision.

Traffic was light. Those who didn't have to venture out into the rain were probably snugged warmly inside their homes. The idea of doing the same lacked the appeal it had presented an hour ago.

Truth be told, when she'd recognized Peter's return address on the mail that had been delivered, she'd dreaded opening it. It had been easier to put it off until she had a free evening to devote to handling her personal correspondence. Hardly the reaction of someone pining for her lost love.

Grimacing, she turned on to St. Ann Street. She never would have described herself as contrary, Charlotte's opinions aside. So why this welter of emotion now, brewing and bubbling inside her? Apparently, she was a bit more temperamental than she'd realized.

She brought her car to a stop in front of her Creole-style house, for once not pausing to take pleasure in the double verandas, the enclosed courtyard. Resting her forehead against the steering wheel, she let the events of the last hour swamp her.

She'd been dumped, in as public a way possible. And as much as it pained her to admit it, her mother had been right about one thing.

She was going to have to start planning just how she was going to deal with it.

Chapter 3

"I come bearin' po'boys." Lucky pushed Jacey's office door open the rest of the way and held up the bag of food, waggling it enticingly.

She didn't look up from the papers she had strewn across her desk. "I'm not hungry."

He came into the office anyway, pushing the door closed with his shoulder. "It's almost closin' time and Joan told me you didn't have lunch. You have to eat. Men like curves on their women, not all bones and angles."

She did glance up then, and the look she gave him would have sent most scurrying out the door. But Lucky considered himself a courageous enough sort. Besides, he happened to know her weaknesses.

"It may surprise you to discover that what men like is not a maxim that dictates my every action."

He made a show of opening the sack, inhaling deeply.

"It may surprise you to discover that these sandwiches are made with Leidenheimer's bread." He saw, and enjoyed, the way her expression changed. "But I forgot. You don't like Ferdis anyway, right?"

"No."

He noted her gaze never left him as he stopped at the curved-leg library table she used when conferring with clients. "Too bad about that. Me, I'm extra hungry today. But I'm not sure I can eat both of these. Maybe I will save the ham with roast beef gravy to eat later."

"Beast."

She could, he noted with sheer male appreciation, move quite quickly when she wanted to. She was out of her seat and had snatched the sandwich from him before he could even finish teasing her with it.

"I guess I could eat something after all."

"And to wash it down…" He reached into the bag and withdrew two beers. He couldn't really imagine Jacey drinking a beer. She was more the wine and champagne type. He was counting on her turning it down, leaving more for him. He happened to know she kept some fancy flavored water in the small ice box tucked beneath the counter.

She snuck a look at the closed door. "I don't want alcohol on the premises, Lucky."

"Relax." He slouched low in one chair, hooked the one across from him with his foot to drag it closer. "Joan was on her way out as I came in. Something about a church dinner." He stretched out, propping his legs on the opposite chair and crossing them at the ankles. The secretary was a straitlaced teetotaler. Her views on the evils of liquor were well known in the office.

"In that case…" Jacey reached out and swiped the second beer from him.

He attempted to hide his dismay. "You don't even like beer. Do you?"

"Probably not, but this will teach you to bring something I do like the next time, won't it?"

Giving in gracefully, he leaned over to twist the top off her bottle, then dealt with his own. "Last night was pretty bad, huh?"

"It was okay." She bit into her sandwich, eyelids sliding shut in real bliss.

Her guarded tone didn't fool him. He had reason to know that any amount of time spent in the company of Charlotte Wheeler could leave lasting ill effects. "You've been holed up in here since dawn this morning, and from the looks of you, you didn't get much sleep last night."

He knew her well enough to recognize the signs. She was wearing what he always thought of as one of her frighteningly capable power suits. The trim-fitting red jacket and skirt might have been sexy if she'd gotten rid of the no-nonsense buttoned-up blouse beneath. She had her hair scraped up into a knot, and wire-rim glasses perched on her nose, which meant she hadn't put her contacts in. He'd always thought it weird that someone with her money hadn't gone for that new eye surgery everyone talked about, until he'd discovered that she was deathly afraid of needles.

"What did Charlotte do this time?" He bit into the sandwich, never taking his eyes off the woman across from him. Interaction between mother and daughter often left Jacey driven and focused for days, as if renewed dedication to her job could alleviate her mother's disapproval.

"Nothing. I've just been busy today, that's all. I've decided to hire some part-time help so I wrote up a job description and ad for the paper. And the fund-raiser last night wasn't a total loss. I picked up a case and I've been preparing a contract. The file arrived this afternoon."

Interest flared. "Tell me about it." He listened intently as she relayed the conversation she'd had with J. Walter Garvey. He'd heard of the man, of course. It would be difficult to live in New Orleans and be ignorant of Garvey Enterprises, although he couldn't say with certainty just exactly what the man's business entailed.

By the time she'd finished, he'd polished off his sandwich, while she'd barely touched her own. Wiping his mouth with a napkin, he reached out to snag his beer with two fingers. "So he's going to decide who to leave his company to based on the dirt you dig up on his grandchildren?"

He had to wait until she'd finished chewing and swallowing her bite of sandwich before she responded. "By my initial calculations his business is estimated in the billions. So I guess you can't blame him for wanting to be sure his successor has the ability to take his place at the helm."

Lucky tipped the bottle to his lips and drank. "Why do I have the feelin' that Garvey wouldn't consider anyone worthy to take over for him?"

She gave a delicate shrug and continued eating. He took a moment to enjoy the sight. There was really no elegant way to eat a po'boy, but she came closer than most to making the task look refined. He liked her best in moments like these, when she forgot the manners that had no doubt been hammered into her from birth, and just enjoyed herself.

There had been a time, when he'd first met her, when he'd been convinced that she was just another deb with a pretty shell, possessing more money than sense. A time when he'd been certain that her insistence on dabbling in private investigative work was going to get her seriously hurt.

But there had been something about her from the first, a competence he hadn't expected, and a hint of vulnerability that shredded him on the rare occasions it peeked through. The first had earned his eventual respect, the second a pesky thread of protectiveness. He'd been far more surprised than she when he'd decided to stay on three years ago. The time he'd spent employed at Wheeler and Associates was the longest he'd ever stuck at anything. Because the realization always filled him with a mild sense of panic, he preferred not thinking about it at all.

Draining his beer, he set it down and eyed hers, which hadn't been touched yet. "How many grandchildren are there?"

"Four. Rupert has three children, two sons and a daughter, all by different women. So I guess they're all really half-siblings. Lianna has one son. The four range in age from twenty-five to thirty-six."

"Do you know them?"

"I've run into all of Rupert's children on occasion at various functions. I don't recognize the name of Lianna's son, Jeffrey Wharton. While she was married she lived in Boston, and apparently the boy bounced back and forth between her and her ex-husband for most of his life. According to the file, he's been living in New Orleans for the last six months."

She slapped his hand just as his fingers would have closed around her bottle. He adopted what he hoped was a wounded expression. "C'mon *cher,* you know you're not goin' to drink that. Don't be mean."

"Yes, I am." To prove it, she lifted the bottle to her lips and took a long pull. Immediately her eyes squeezed shut, and she choked a little. "That's…" She hauled in a deep breath, smoothed her expression. "That's excellent."

He laughed out loud, delighted with her. "It's an acquired taste, and one I wouldn't have thought to your likin'. By all means, finish it."

"I intend to." She'd do just that to prove a point, and damned if he wasn't going to enjoy watching her. Taking a more cautious sip the next time, she managed to swallow without grimacing. "Thank you for the sandwich. I guess I have been a bit single-minded today."

Lucky stood, began gathering up the wrappers and shoving them back in the bag. "You mean uptight? *Oui,* just a bit." He, on the other hand, had come to work feeling loose and relaxed. A long night of steamy sex had that effect on a man. He would have suggested that she engage in the same, but given her choice in male companions, he doubted her experience would produce similar results. She tended to choose men who were little more than empty suits, all surface polish with no real substance beneath. Although she'd broken away from her high-society upbringing in her choice of careers, she didn't seem able to shake it when it came to the men in her life.

He stood, wadded the bag in his hand and banked it into the wastebasket. Noticing the way she was working her shoulder, he moved to stand behind her. "Here, let me." When she would have batted his hands away, he dug his fingers into the tight muscles, eliciting a groan.

"How do you do that?"

"We all have our talents. Yours is turnin' oversized bikers into eunuchs, and mine is loosenin' up tight muscles." He used his thumb to rub along her nape. "You're all knots."

"I tossed and turned most of the night." She let her head loll, allowing him better access. "I woke up stiff."

Her lack of sleep could no doubt be laid squarely at her mother's doorstep, but bringing up the woman's name would just have her tensing again. "You need to learn how to relax."

"So you always say." She rolled her shoulders. He thought the muscles there were already becoming more pliable. "M-mm, with your talent, you could become a professional at this."

"Fa'true?" He pretended to consider it. "Maybe I'll just do that. I could stop slavin' away for you on that paltry salary you pay me and open my own business." He pretended not to hear the sound she made in response. "Yeah, I'm thinkin' of buying a van with equipment inside it. I could make housecalls first thing in the mornin' to provide wake-up massages for the stressed out-women of the city. I could call it…Loosen up with Lucky."

She tilted her head back to look at him. "Why not? I know of some dog groomers who work that way. They go to the customers' homes and provide the service in the back of their vans. You might even want to offer some of the same services they do—I'm sure some of the 'clients' you'd acquire could benefit from a good flea dip."

Lucky's chuckle joined her laughter, even as he lowered his face to hers to growl in mock menace, "You're a cruel woman, *cher,* to trample a man's dreams that way."

"Dreams? Don't you mean fantasies?"

"*Oui,* and now I have a far different fantasy in mind, one that involves…" He broke off as he heard a sound in the outer office. In the next moment the door to Jacey's office was pushed open, and a man filled the doorway.

Time stilled for an instant as the three of them froze. In the next second Jacey straightened abruptly, in a move designed to dislodge Lucky's hands. He was just contrary enough to keep them in place. "Brummond." His fingers resumed their kneading motion. "Haven't seen you around for a while." His grin was as careless as his words. "Can't say I've missed you."

Peter Brummond stepped into the office, his gaze first taking in the placement of Lucky's hands, then the bottle in Jacey's hand.

"Jacinda." The word was stiff. "I apologize if I'm interrupting."

"We just finished a working dinner." Jacey tried to rise, but Lucky's placement behind her chair prevented it. She turned and shot him a telling glance. "It's after five, Lucky. Lock up on your way out, will you?"

As a dismissal it was fairly obvious. There was no reason for it to burn the way it did. "Are you sure?" As far as he could tell, dropping Brummond a few months ago had been one of Jacey's smartest moves. "We really weren't finished here."

Her smile was tight, but her eyes held a plea, one he couldn't help but respond to. "I'm sure."

He didn't have to feign his reluctance. He didn't know what Brummond's presence here after all this time meant, but he was pretty damn certain it couldn't be good. Slowly, he let his hands drop from her shoulders and rounded the table. The other man stepped aside, allowing him room to pass, then shut the door behind him.

"What was that all about?"

If she hadn't known better, she would have thought there was a note of jealousy in Peter's voice, but that was ridiculous. Peter was getting married. He'd made his choice. Both of them had.

"Please sit down." The graciousness in her voice would have made her mother proud. "I must admit I'm a bit surprised to see you, though."

The man had the grace to flush. He lowered himself to a chair opposite Jacey's. "Believe me, I know I've handled this badly. I wanted to talk to you a dozen times, but I just...I didn't know what to say. Or how to say it."

"I understand congratulations are in order. Have the two of you set a date yet?" She had the distant realization that she'd never seen Peter Brummond so discomfited. It would have been satisfying if she weren't so intensely uncomfortable herself.

"We're...it will be a small ceremony. Private. That's why Mother insisted on the engagement affair. You know how she likes a party."

What Audrey Brummond loved most, Jacey recalled, was having the spotlight on her and her family. She couldn't imagine that a private wedding ceremony had been Peter's mother's idea, hence the engagement party.

Peter fidgeted in his seat. His blond good looks were just as polished as she remembered, saved from conventional handsomeness by a chin that was a shade too weak. "This thing with Celeste…well, it took me by surprise, too. That is, it all happened so quickly…"

"You and I were no longer seeing each other," Jacey put in smoothly. "You had a right to date other women."

His expression eased a fraction. "That's true. I still felt though, that as a courtesy I should have informed you, but there never seemed an opportune moment."

"The announcement did take me aback," Jacey conceded in masterful understatement. Never had Miss Denoue's deportment classes come in so handy. She was hardly tempted at all to brain the man with the paperweight on the desk behind her. "But we've known each other a long time. I'm happy for you, Peter. I'll be there at the engagement party with the rest of your friends wishing you and your fiancée all the best."

For some reason his face grew pained. "About that…Mother told me that she'd sent you an invitation. And of course I want you there, you have to believe that. But it's bound to be a trifle awkward, don't you think?"

Little bubbles of anger fired through her veins as comprehension washed over her. Jacey's fingers tightened on the bottle in her hand. The insufferable jerk hadn't come to apologize at all. Oh, he'd done an excellent job with the downcast eyes and contrite expression, but the man had always been a master of getting what he wanted.

And it was obvious that what he wanted was for her to stay far away from his engagement party.

Because the temptation to use the bottle on him was growing too strong, she set it aside. The polite thing to do, of course, was to agree. In their world, appearances were everything. Her absence from the event would certainly ease things for him and his fiancée.

The fact that it would almost certainly worsen things for her wasn't a matter either of them were supposed to discuss.

"Awkward? Do you really think so?" She hoped the smile she sent him revealed none of the smoldering anger she was experiencing. "I tend to think we'd do a better job of quieting the gossips if people see us together. Then they'll realize we remain friends and the rumors will die down."

One of his hands went to his jacket pocket, a sure sign of his nerves. She could hear the faint jingle of keys. "Of course, that's logical. And that's exactly what I've told Celeste. But she's a bit on the shy side, and she's afraid the whole matter will become uncomfortable. She's not as adept with these situations as you and I are."

"Oh, dear." She hoped her tone sounded appropriately sympathetic. It was difficult to summon real empathy for a man she could quite cheerfully push in front of an oncoming bus. "I wouldn't distress your fiancée for the world, but I really think it's best if I made an appearance. You know how pesky the rumor mill can be. And while your marriage will end the talk about you, I think my absence from the party will fan the flames of gossip about me. And I'm really not willing to undergo it, Peter. I'd hope you'd want to spare me that."

There was a sort of remote pleasure in watching the man squirm. Quite literally. "Of course not. That wasn't my intention at all."

"Good." She smiled at him, rose. She wasn't sure how much longer she could maintain this charade. "So I'll see you...when was the date again?"

"This Saturday." He was slower to get to his feet. Having failed at what he'd come here for, he was clearly not anxious to leave. But he was too much of a gentleman to press his point. A shallow, weak-willed, stuffy mama's boy, but a gentleman, nonetheless. "You're certainly welcome to come. I hope I didn't give the impression that you weren't."

The man couldn't even manage to imbue the words with a scrap of sincerity. That made it almost easy for Jacey to nod and say, "Wonderful. I wouldn't miss it for the world."

Five minutes later when Lucky stuck his head in the door, his eyes widened comically when he saw her drain the bottle of now-warm beer and slam it on the table. Catching his gaze, she lied, "Delightful. Too bad you didn't bring a few more. Did you lock the front door?"

"About ten minutes too late, but yeah." He came into the room, his face quizzical.

"Good." She pushed away from the table and went to her desk. "I'm going to stay a while longer, but there's no reason for you to hang around. You're always whining about me working you too hard. I'll see you tomorrow."

She looked down sightlessly at the file folders arranged in neat piles on her desk. What she needed right now was to get lost in her work. There were still numerous details about the Garvey case to work out. It would probably work best if she and Lucky divided up the four potential heirs and then consulted daily on their findings. Although perhaps it would be smarter to…

With two arms braced on her desk, Lucky leaned toward her. She hadn't even heard his approach. The man moved like a cat. "What happened?"

Striving to recapture the insouciance she'd managed with Brummond, she forced herself to meet his gaze. "You mean with Peter? Nothing at all. Why do you ask?"

But unlike the other man, the cool tone didn't seem to fool Lucky. His dark gaze intent, he said softly, "Don't lie to me, Jacey. You don't want to tell me, then say that. But no lies. I think we owe each other better, *n'est ce pas?*"

Feeling a bit ashamed, she gave up the pretense of interest in the files and met his gaze. "Peter is getting married. Soon. As a matter of fact, there's going to be an engagement party for him and his fiancée this weekend."

His face was watchful. "He came here to tell you that?"

The knots were back in her shoulders. She leaned back in her chair, suddenly weary. "I would have found out for myself if I had opened the invitation that came to my house. As it turns out, I learned from my mother last night." She made a face. "She's not happy that I let him slip through my fingers."

"So…what was he doin' here?"

She gave a humorless smile. "Well, that depends on your interpretation, I imagine. Since I'm not in a particularly charitable mood, I'd say he was dispatched by his fiancée to make sure my appearance didn't mar her special night."

Pushing away from the desk, he rounded the corner and propped his hips against the side. Arms folded, he inquired, "And you told him...what?"

"That I wasn't willing to give the gossips more fuel. Damn." Lucky's eyes widened a fraction as the unfamiliar curse passed her lips. "I'd rather face a ten-inch needle than put myself through facing all those people at his party." Every one of them would be watching, judging her every expression and word. Just the thought had dread snaking through her belly.

"So don't go."

"I don't have a choice." Hearing the words, she corrected them. "I mean, I have choices, but I don't like either of them. When it comes down to it, I refuse to allow myself to be the target of speculation. I'll go, hold my head up and put on the show of my life. And I'll detest every minute of it." She met his gaze. "I guess that means I have more of my mother in me than I thought."

"It means you have pride. There's nothin' wrong with that."

As awful as the beer had tasted, Jacey wished she had another. There was a sort of pleasant haze drifting over her, blunting the edges of her emotions. She'd never been much of a drinker. "What would you do if it were you?"

"I'd do exactly what you plan to. People will talk regardless. At least this way you can direct what they're going to say."

She considered that, before nodding. "Exactly. I'm not going to take my mother's advice, though. She gave me a carefully prepared list of eligible bachelors from which to choose an escort. I had the impression they also met her requirements for a son-in-law."

His face went impassive. "For once, Charlotte and I agree on something. If people think you're involved with someone else you remove the drama from the scene. You don't need her list, though. I'll take you myself."

A wave of warmth flooded her at the mere thought. Showing up with Lucky in tow wouldn't stem talk about her, it would only stoke it. But there'd be no pitying looks directed her way with him by her side. Just because she was immune to his brand of charm herself, didn't mean she was unaware of his effect on most other females. He'd be fortunate to escape the party without landing several propositions from the women, and more than a few hostile exchanges from the men.

A smile played across her lips. It would be almost worth suffering her mother's wrath just to watch the impact he'd make accompanying her. With a reluctant shake of her head, though, she dismissed the idea. "You'd hate that sort of thing."

"So you will owe me, *c'est tout.*" The wicked glint in his eye gave lie to his nonchalant shrug. "What's a favor among friends?"

"I'd hate to guess what you'd demand in return. No, I'll think of something." Something, she hoped, that would leave her with a measure of dignity intact. And if it also included a way to maim Peter, she'd consider that a bonus. The situation was uncomfortable, but hardly rose to the level of catastrophic, no matter what her mother feared.

All she had to do between now and Saturday was to come up with a way to convince her friends and acquaintances that she was unaffected by the whole turn of events.

Piece of cake.

Chapter 4

Lucky walked down Bourbon Street, taking in the familiar sights. T-Bone was on his regular corner, clad in silver clothes with silver paint covering his face, neck and hands. The pose he struck was so still he could have passed for a discarded store mannequin. He was one of many street performers who dotted the corners, depending on the largesse of tourists for their living. By the looks of the small crowd gathering, T-Bone was having a good night.

Jamming his hands into the pockets of his jeans, Lucky strolled up and stared at the unmoving man. T-Bone did an excellent job of ignoring his presence.

"How does he stand so still?" one woman wondered aloud. "He hardly seems to be breathing."

"Oh, that's easy, ma'am." Lucky smiled wickedly. "See, T-Bone here is deaf and dumb. Mostly just dumb." He thought, he was almost certain, he saw the man's eyes flicker. Warming up to his story, he donned a thick good-ol'-boy accent and told the crowd, "How I know that is, we're cousins, him and me. You can't see the family resemblance 'cuz of the silver paint and all. Not that we look all that much alike because, well," he looked around at the rapt people, and lowered his voice conspiratorially, "T-Bone here is the ugly one in the family. Our granny used to have to tie a pork chop around his neck just to get the dogs to play with him." There was a snicker, and T-Bone's lips compressed a fraction. "Plus he's lazy as a tarred hog, so standin' around on street corners is about all that boy is up for."

"Damn you, Boucher, keep on trash-talking me and I'll stomp a mudhole in you." T-Bone dropped his pose and stepped down from the upside-down bucket he was perched on. The tourists, giving him a wide berth now, hurried away. The man looked after them mournfully. "Now why'd you want and go and do that? Some people appreciate art."

"So maybe they're headin' for a museum. Hey, have you seen Remy today?"

T-Bone gave him a crafty look. "What's the information worth to you?"

"I'll let you keep those bills in that box there." The cigar box in front of T-Bone's bucket was filled with a few bills and coins. He knew the bulk of the money would already have been placed for safe-keeping in an inner pocket sewed inside T-Bone's shirt.

The other man made a sound of derision, but he was careful to shove the box behind him with one foot. "Yeah, I saw Remy earlier. Maybe an hour ago. He was in some hurry, too. I think he was working."

Lucky nodded. At ten o'clock at night, he'd expected no less. "Which direction was he headed?"

With his eye on a couple of pairs of tourists headed in their direction, T-Bone abruptly lost interest in the conversation. Climbing back up on the pail to assume his position, he jerked a thumb in the opposite direction and said, "That way. Now beat it before this next group gets here. And don't be telling people no more that we're related, either. Out of all the lies you told there, that was the worst."

"From what I hear of my *pauvre defante maman*, we just might be." Lucky chuckled at the man's muttered epithet and headed down the street and around the corner in the direction he had indicated.

The streets were still full of people. Tourism would be brisk for another couple of months, then slow until Mardi Gras. Unlike some of the city's residents, Lucky didn't mind sharing his city with the visitors. He understood their fascination with the place. There was a slight air of decadence to the city that never failed to intrigue. Beneath a thin veneer of polish there was an aura of decay that could never be completely disguised. The city fathers preferred to believe it didn't exist. But as one who'd spent more than his share of time living on these streets, he could attest that it did. In spite of it, or perhaps because of it, he'd been drawn to the city from the first time he'd come here from bayou country when he was nineteen. He'd never wanted to live anyplace else, although there had been plenty of times when just living had been a constant struggle.

Lucky looked up in response to some calls overhead, and took a second to grin appreciatively at the sight of scantily clad women enticing passersby in to the strip club where they worked. Their faces were painted as garishly as the flickering neon sign out front. They couldn't tempt him, however. He needed to find his friend, and the sooner the better.

He stopped at a corner where an elderly black man was playing a mournful jazz tune on the sax. He waited until he was finished, and set the instrument down. "Lucky. Where y'at?"

"Hey, Grayson. I'm lookin' for Remy. Did he come by?"

"Saw him a while ago. Looked to be in a hurry, too." The old man's wrinkled face took on a thoughtful air. "Maybe forty-five minutes ago. Headed that way."

Lucky's gaze followed the old man's gnarled finger. Dropping some money into his box, he continued on his way. "Next time bring me foldin' money, not rollin' money, Boucher," the man called after him. He hunched a shoulder in response.

The farther he strayed from the tourist destinations, the narrower the streets became. Many of the streetlights had been broken out long ago. What appeared as a slightly seedy reminder of a bygone era in the French Quarter deteriorated into indisputable roughness in this neighborhood. There was a time when Lucky had belonged on these same streets, had known them as well as he knew his own reflection in the mirror. Even after three years, they still felt like home.

He stepped into the street to avoid tripping over the body sprawled across the sidewalk in front of a tavern. In doing so, he almost missed Remy altogether. A barely audible sound caught his attention. He turned and

scanned the area. Spying the alley ten yards away, he
backtracked and crossed close enough to it to peer in.

Two men were on the ground rolling in the dirt, trading blows. Although the interior of the alley was too
dark to identify either of them, Lucky did recognize his
friend's style. He sent a quick glance up and down the
street to assure himself there was no law enforcement
in the area, and then stepped into the alley. Leaning a
shoulder against a bordering building, he waited.

The other man with Remy was no slouch when it
came to street fighting, Lucky noted. His friend seemed
to have his hands full. He winced a little when the
stranger sent a fist into Remy's face, nodded in approval
when his friend countered with a double eye-gouge.
Niceties of battle were rarely used in back alleys. Lucky
should know. He'd spent enough time in them.

His casual air was shattered a moment later when the
stranger rolled away to pick up a large brick. One moment he was raising it threateningly above Remy's head,
and the next he froze.

"Not a good idea, *mon ami*." Lucky pressed the tip
of his knife closer against the man's throat. "I suggest
you set it down. Slowly." When it appeared the stranger
needed a bit more convincing, he exerted enough pressure to have blood welling from beneath the blade. With
exaggerated care, the man set the brick to the ground.

Looking at his friend, Lucky inquired, "How much
does he owe?"

Remy wiped a smear of blood away from his mouth,
and grunted. "Two hundred. But you should just leave
me to finish him with that brick."

"Two hundred?" The man started toward Remy until

the pressure of the knife stopped him. "That whore wasn't worth the hundred I got quoted, much less two."

"It's an extra hundred for my trouble, Cap." The familiar address was its own kind of slur, uttered as it was while Remy was expertly removing the man's wallet, extracting the money he sought. "It's not healthy in these parts to welch on a debt owed. These are people it doesn't pay to antagonize."

"You're gettin' off easy," Lucky affirmed. He stepped away, keeping the knife ready in case the man decided to be stupid or brave.

The stranger cast a sullen glance at the two of them before taking the opportunity to back away. When he'd exited the alley, Lucky wiped the knife blade on his pants leg and bent to replace it in the sheath strapped above his right ankle. "How long you been doing collections?"

Remy gave the discarded brick a kick and lifted a shoulder. "A while. Marcus took off one step ahead of the cops and Nemo's in jail. They needed someone to fill in, and the pay's better, you know?" He patted his pocket, where he'd stuck the extra hundred. "Anyway, I was in your old job nearly three years, and it wasn't going anywhere. This is a step up in the organization."

There was a time when Lucky would have thought the same thing. But right now he could only wonder what would have happened to his friend if he hadn't found him when he had. He knew better than to voice that question aloud, however. Remy would be no more open to advice than he would be himself.

They fell into step together and left the alley. People could be forgiven for believing them brothers. They were similar in height, build and coloring. But it was a past, rather than blood, that connected them. They'd grown up on the same bayou. Had attended the same schools, displayed the same curiosity about what lay beyond the swamp. They'd left their families for the city together.

Remy attempted to smooth his hair. The most obvious difference between them was that he'd always taken much more care with his appearance than did Lucky. "Where were you headin', anyway?"

"Came lookin' for you. Your family has been trying to reach you. When they couldn't, they called me."

Remy grunted. "Lost my cell last night while I was chasin' down another lowlife. Had to call the company today and cancel my plan. I suppose I'll have to go in tomorrow and pick out another one." Attempting to brush off his white shirt, he inquired, "Who called you? What's wrong?"

"It's your *Tante* Martine. She's in the hospital."

Remy stopped, blanched. "What's wrong?" Like Lucky, Remy hadn't grown up with his parents. Martine and her late husband Louis had raised him.

"It's her diabetes again, but she'll be okay." Lucky clapped him on the shoulder. "She always is. But maybe you should go."

His friend nodded. "I'll have to talk to Vinny, let him know what's goin' on. I don't want him to think I split like Marco. This is a good job. I can't afford to lose it."

For an instant, Lucky was tempted to tell him of the opening at Wheeler and Associates. Remy would be no less experienced than he'd been when he'd gotten his license. But the moment came and passed, and still he held his tongue. His friend knew about the work he did, but not for whom. As a matter of fact, he'd never mentioned Jacey to him at all.

Rather than delving too deeply into the reasons for his reticence, he changed the subject. "They took Martine to the medical center in Thibodaux. You can take my cell with you until you get back, if you want."

But Remy was shaking his head. "Thanks, but you need it. I'll call my cousin from a pay phone before I head home tonight. Tomorrow after I find out more about her condition, I'll let you know."

Lucky nodded, recognizing the worry on his friend's face. Martine was as close to a mother as Remy had. He had reason to know that family was doubly precious to those who had grown up with so little of it. The two men said their goodbyes, and he stood for a moment, watching his friend hurry down the darkened street. He hoped Vinny Tomsino was as understanding as Remy expected. When Lucky had worked for him, the man had never struck him as overly concerned with anything other than turning a profit.

With the memory came a wave of déjà vu that transported him back to the time not so long ago when he'd been spending more than his share of time in dark alleys just like the one where he'd found Remy. Perhaps the biggest difference between the two of them was that Remy still expected more. Lucky never had.

No one was more surprised than he at the turn of events that had him working in an upscale neighborhood for a woman he would have normally never even spoken to.

Which only went to show that Lady Fate, she was a fickle woman indeed.

* * *

It was one of life's little ironies that the more Jacey dreaded a particular event, the faster it seemed to approach. After Peter's visit, Lucky had been dispatched to Rhode Island to check on Jeffrey Wharton's college career. He'd been gone three days and she refused to admit, even to herself, that she missed him. There was something to be said for having someone around to bounce ideas off of. Lucky was great for that. Of course, he was often more blunt than necessary with his opinions about her thoughts, but at least he provided a sounding board.

She'd divided her time finishing the Kenning case and combing the databases for information on Rupert Garvey's children. It had only taken the better part of an afternoon to discover the locales where Cheryl Kenning could be found, along with the usual times. Once she'd assured herself of the information, she passed it on to the Kenning grandparents. What they did with it from that point was no concern of Jacey's. If Lucky had been around, she was certain he would have had an opinion on that, as well.

She'd left the office that Saturday afternoon with a sense of accomplishment. One case had been neatly tied up and she'd gotten a good start on the newest one. But by early evening that feeling of well-being had long since vanished. Staring blindly at the contents of her closet, Jacey wished mightily that she'd saved just a little of her brainpower that week for figuring out a way to avoid the engagement party altogether.

Heaving a sigh, she tugged a dress from its hanger and stepped into it. The reason she'd spent as little time as possible thinking about this moment was precisely because she knew there was no way out of it. Not for her. The evening promised to be embarrassing and awkward, but it wasn't likely to kill her. She'd show up, mingle long enough to speak to all her acquaintances, join in a toast to the happy couple, then leave with concealed haste while the tongues wagged behind her.

She spent several minutes pulling her hair up into an intricate knot atop her head. Then, surveying herself critically in the mirror, she freed two tendrils to frame her face. Checking the tiny dome clock on her dresser, she donned earrings, a ring and necklace, sprayed herself with perfume, and, straightening her shoulders, checked her appearance one last time. Her expression was as excited as if she was on her way to the gallows. And why had she chosen this dress? The bright blue fabric clung to her curves in a way that usually made her feel confident and sexy, but now seemed a little too daring. Tugging the neckline to a more discreet level, she sneaked another look at the clock, trying to gauge whether she had enough time to change. The doorbell rang.

The sound had her freezing. Surely, surely it couldn't be her mother. But even while she repeated the litany to herself as she went to the door, she knew she was wrong. After a brief conversation earlier this week, Jacey had been dodging her calls. Charlotte had probably not trusted her to show up on her own.

Hand on the doorknob, she hesitated. She wouldn't put it past her mother to show up with one of the men from the list in tow, presenting her daughter with a fait accompli. Narrowing her gaze suspiciously, she withdrew her hand and opted to use the peephole instead. What she saw there had her opening the door hastily.

"Lucky! You're back."

With one shoulder leaning against the doorjamb, he shot her a lazy smile. "*Oui.* I was tempted to stay longer and milk the expense account for a lengthy bout of relaxation, but…I was in Rhode Island. Nothing relaxin' about that." Pushing away, he straightened and brushed by her to enter, sweeping her figure with his gaze as he did so. "You're looking…remarkable."

So are you. The words leaped through her mind, almost tumbled from her lips before she caught herself. She'd never seen him so dressed up, and she couldn't help wondering what the occasion was this time. He was wearing black dress slacks, a collarless black shirt and a matching jacket without lapels. With his dark hair carelessly brushed back, he looked like a fallen dark angel.

"You must have gone shopping on your trip." She arched a brow at him. "I hope not on the company's dime."

"*Non.* I do have something in my closet besides T-shirts and jeans. I just don't choose to wear them often." He threw her a wicked glance over his shoulder as he walked into the living room. "Another thing you'll owe me. The debt is mountin', and the evenin' hasn't even begun yet."

She stared at him, uncomprehending. Then a flicker of understanding filtered through. "The…evening?"

He turned to face her, hands slipped casually into his pants pockets. "Brummond's engagement party. You didn't say what time it began, so I just took a guess and headed over. Figured if I was early we could always catch up on the case."

Thoughts in a whirl, she blinked at him. "Um, it starts at seven. But I distinctly remember telling you I was goin' alone."

"And I distinctly remember tellin' you that I'd take you." He cocked an eyebrow at her. "What's the matter, *cher?* Did you give in and call one of the guys on your mother's list, after all?"

Temper snapped up her spine. "Certainly not!"

"Good. That's good. So what's the problem? You'll make an appearance with a man, stop the worst of the rumors. People might still talk, but they won't be feelin' sorry for you." His gaze was sober, direct. "Pity can have far sharper edges than malice, *n'est ce pas?*"

She stared at him, unable to voice her agreement. But it was there, nonetheless. Despite their differences, despite their backgrounds, he could stun her at times with his insight. It was a curiosity of fate that nowhere else, not the private all-girl academy she'd attended, not the Ivy League college, had she ever met anyone who could so effortlessly pluck her thoughts from her mind and utter them with with such certain logic.

She assessed him with new eyes. He'd taken far more care with his appearance than she'd ever noted before. He was also clean-shaven, and she was fairly certain he never shaved on the weekends. And in the end, despite the warning alarm shrilling inside her, it was that simple consideration that decided her.

"Sure you're up for this?" she asked dubiously. "People are going to be even more interested in you than they are in me."

He lifted a shoulder. "How tough can it be? Bunch of rich people drinkin' and talkin' too much, thinkin' too little. So." He looked her over critically. "Are you ready? It's comin' on seven now."

Before she could think better of it, she nodded, headed for the coat closet. "I'll get my coat."

"Why wear a dress like that, only to cover it with a coat?" Lucky caught her by the arm, turned her gently toward the door. "This evenin' is about appearances. Let's do somethin' about yours." Jacey felt his hands in her hair, and before she could guess his intentions, he'd released the hairstyle she'd taken pains with, dropping the pins on the floor. Then he threaded his fingers through her hair, shook the strands free.

Catching a look at herself in the hallway mirror, Jacey hissed in an annoyed breath. Her hair was as mussed as if she'd just crawled out of bed. "Dammit!" She slapped his hands away. "Now I'll just be later trying to fix it."

"You don't need to fix it. It's fine." He reached out, hooked a finger in the neckline of her dress, and tugged it a couple inches lower. Then he grinned at the strangled sound she made. "Now you look fine, too. Re-e-al fine."

"Boucher, you are really living dangerously." Ineffectually trying to smooth her hair and straighten her dress, she felt herself being nudged, ever so discreetly, toward the door.

"*Mais, oui.* I am a dangerous man, Jacey. Haven't you figured that out yet?"

The front door snicked closed behind them, the quiet sound punctuating his words. A sliver of unease skated over her skin. Sometimes, at the oddest moments, she was vividly reminded of the first time she'd met Lucky. The instant wariness his appearance in her office had elicited, and yes, the prickle of fear. His affable charm could make her forget for long periods of time about both. But it paid to remember. Lucky Boucher *was* a dangerous man, in more ways than one. That knowledge stemmed from an instinctive, rather than a logical level.

She'd done a background check on him before hiring him, but it had turned up amazingly little. For a twenty-five-year-old resident of the state, there had been surprisingly little information to be gathered about him. Certainly nothing she'd uncovered had mentioned the origins of that hint of menace that could appear and then vanish so swiftly, a person was inclined to think she'd imagined it.

And it was increasingly difficult to recall it under the steady stream of patter he was treating her to right now. "You're fortunate to be ridin' in style tonight. My car was in the shop this week. I need a raise to pay the mechanic's ransom demands."

"Very smooth, the way you slipped that in," she noted as he opened the door for her. "But the answer is no. Why don't you break down and get yourself something newer? It would save you a fortune in repair costs."

The outrage on his face was comical. "Trade her in? Trade her? Would a father exchange his only child? Would you part with one of your precious antiques because it is old?"

She wanted, badly, to smile. Firming her lips, she got in the car. He shut the door after her, caressing the hood protectively as he rounded the vehicle. "What is this strange fixation some men have for their cars?" she asked, when he'd gotten inside.

"It's not a fixation," he corrected her, checking traffic before pulling out into the street. "It's respect. Treat a vehicle with respect and it treats you well right back."

"Is that what it was treating you with when it stalled in the middle of the four-lane earlier this week?" she asked, tongue firmly in cheek.

He made a sound like a growl. "Cars, like women, can be temperamental, no matter how excellent the care they receive."

She rolled her eyes. "I'm not touching that one. Do you know where we're going?" She recited the address for him.

"I know the area." He turned the corner. "Houses there are similar to your mother's, right? Too much grass and brick and not enough personality."

"That's an accurate description, I guess." Nerves began jittering in her veins. To calm them, she asked, "What did you find out about Jeffrey Wharton?"

"Well, it was an interestin' few days. Seems ol' Jeffrey is a *couillion,* an idiot who has bounced through six colleges in five years. From his grades it's difficult to understand how he ever got accepted to that many in the first place. His family must have paid through the nose each time to grease the way."

"Well, his mother certainly has the money. His father, too, although they've been divorced for years now. He's a high-powered trial lawyer in Boston."

Lucky nodded. "He majored in international affairs. His grades at Brown weren't that bad. Maybe he finally decided to buckle down. It was his other activities that had university authorities lookin' at him."

"Such as?"

Lucky accelerated, easily passing a slower moving

van and slipping into the lane ahead of it. "Our guy had himself a pretty lucrative sideline. He was a major drug dealer on campus. Makes me wonder who his connection was, to get that big, that fast. It's not as though he grew up in Providence."

Jacey reflected on that. "How good is your source?"

"The best." Lucky grinned. "Among others, I heard this from Wharton's bitter ex-girlfriend. And I talked to enough others to figure she was tellin' the truth, at least about the drugs. We'll have to take her word on his, ah, sexual appetites."

"I haven't picked up any hints of his involvement in drugs now that he's returned home, but I've only just gotten started. He's working at a low-level position in his grandfather's company. From the sounds of it, he's a glorified mail sorter."

"Livin' within his means?"

"It's hard to tell. He's staying with Lianna now, driving and wrecking her vehicles. If he's throwing money around he's doing it on things other than rent and cars. It should be easy enough to trace, though. He doesn't get his hands on his trust fund for another six months."

"But he's managed finally to get a degree that could loosely tie in with Garvey Shipping. And he's got his foot in the door there, so I'd say either he or his mother are buckin' for grandad's attention on the youngest descendant."

"Given his activities in college he'd be a pretty bad bet to be given any say in running the company." There was no way to tell who his drug connections had been, but the fact that he had any sounded a death knell for his future in the shipping business. Even if he was clean now, he'd be too vulnerable to powerful dealers wanting to use the company to transport their trade.

"Think I should continue checking the other campuses he spent time enrolled at?" The car's powerful engine roared as Lucky blithely ignored the speed limit posted on the freeway.

"Not yet. I'm pretty sure this information would automatically erase him from Walter Garvey's consideration." Which left them with three other grandchildren to focus on. "The oldest of Rupert's children is Stephen, who's thirty-six, married, with three small children. He's a stockbroker. The FTC investigated him two years ago regarding an insider trading allegation, but nothing ever stuck."

Lucky frowned. "If Garvey is lookin' for someone with the expertise to run his company, a stockbroker isn't going to have much."

"I'm sure he already knows what his grandchildren's work experience is. I think he's looking for someone with the brains and a relatively stain-free past who would be willing to learn the business from the bottom up."

He gave a shrug. "Then Stephen makes the short list, at least for now. An investigation by the Federal Trade Commission isn't proof of wrongdoin'."

Jacey continued. "Amanda is next. At thirty-three she owns a headhunter firm, supplying potential employees to hospitals across the South. Her company has tripled its size in the last five years alone, so she's obviously got a mind for business."

When she stopped, he prompted, "But?"

She gave an uncomfortable shrug. "I don't know if this should count against her, but she's been married four times and is engaged again. Fortunately, there are no kids."

"Ah." Lucky's tone was mocking. "Obviously a romantic."

"Apparently you can be a shrewd businesswoman and still have unfortunate taste in men. At least two of her former husbands were charged with domestic violence."

"So she bears some more lookin' into. Who's the last of them?"

"The other half brother is Mark. He's thirty, a corporate lawyer, and recently divorced. His ex-wife is a friend of mine. They just had a baby a couple years ago. He's worked for Garvey Enterprises since he passed the bar."

"You'd think Walter Garvey would already know all he needs to about him, then."

"Maybe." It depended, she supposed, on just how often their paths crossed. From what the older man had said, it hadn't seemed as though he knew any of his descendants well. On the other hand, he might already be considering Mark and had hired Jacey to make sure he hadn't overlooked anything. "We'll continue to check on Wharton's current activities, but it's doubtful J. Walter would approve of him, given his past. We can concentrate most of our efforts on Rupert's three children."

"Will any of the Garvey clan be there tonight?"

She tried to think. "It's hard to say. Lianna is an acquaintance of my mother's. They belong to the same church, serve on the board together. It's possible. Peter's mother knows her well, too. I've only met Rupert once or twice, but I haven't seen him around much in recent years." Of course, she'd been avoiding the social engagements her mother loved as much as possible lately. "Mark is a friend of Peter's. He was probably invited."

She stopped then, recognizing the neighborhood they were entering. The large estates were set well back from the road, some almost hidden by trees. The Brummond mansion was completely unobscured, however, save for the wrought-iron fence that ran around its perimeter. Her throat dried as Lucky slowed at the gate.

The guard stooped to peer in the window that Lucky lowered. "Invitation please."

It occurred to Jacey for the first time that not only had she forgotten the invitation, but she hadn't even thought to bring her purse. Lucky's arrival had completely shaken her usually organized pattern.

Unless one considered the failure to bring the invitation thus possibly being barred admittance as some sort of Freudian slip.

She leaned forward to look past the window. "I'm sorry, I've forgotten it. Please check your guest list for Jacinda Wheeler."

"Miss Wheeler?" The man peered more closely, then smiled. "Good evening, ma'am. Nice to see you again. Hope you enjoy yourself tonight."

Her thank-you sounded weak, even to her own ears. Lucky drove the car down the wide circular drive and the closer he got to the house, the tighter the knots drew in her stomach. If it had been possible to fast forward through the next few hours, she would have.

Flipping down the visor, she checked her appearance in the mirror, aghast at her reflection. For the duration of the trip she'd forgotten Lucky's hand in her dishevelment. With frantic movements, she attempted to restore her hair to order.

Her attempt was thwarted when he reached by her and pushed the visor back up. "Leave it. It looks better this way."

She sent him a killing glance, then tried to straighten her neckline. "Thanks to you, I look like a slut."

He brought the car to a halt before the front steps. "You say that like it's a bad thing."

She was saved from answering by the valet opening her door, helping her out from the vehicle. Walking to the door, she felt, rather than saw Lucky join her. She drew in a deep breath and tried to ignore the cloak of trepidation threatening to smother her. This was ridiculous. She was a healthy, well-adjusted adult. The party might turn out to be unpleasant, but it would hardly be life-altering.

Still, as a uniformed maid swung the door open, and the sounds of the party spilled out, Jacey was honest enough to admit that she was glad she hadn't had to come alone.

Having even Lucky by her side was better than nothing.

Chapter 5

Lucky gave a mental whistle as they walked past the maid and headed for the living room. The floors were marble, the walls were lined with what even his untrained eye could tell was expensive artwork, and the chandelier overhead threw off enough prisms from its hanging crystals to blind a man.

Still, he found himself comparing the place unfavorably to Jacey's refurbished Creole-style house. The grandeur couldn't even remotely come close to capturing the cozy elegance of her home. This was a place for show rather than one suited to live in, not unlike Jacey's childhood home. He much preferred a house that didn't shout No Trespassing, but given his choice in apartments, he supposed his standards weren't especially high.

To their immediate right was a living room filled

with people. He slanted a glance at Jacey. Although her expression was a smooth polite mask, he could read her underlying nerves in the set of her shoulders. Deliberately, he took a step closer, his lips brushing her hair as he whispered in her ear, "Does it help to picture them all naked?"

He could have sworn he heard her choke back a laugh. She turned her face toward his to murmur, "None of your outrageousness, Boucher. Your appearance is supposed to help my cause, not make it worse." Seeing an older woman bearing down on him, he didn't answer, but when Jacey would have moved away, he moved with her, maintaining their proximity. He saw by the woman's expression that she hadn't missed the air of intimacy between them. Good. A sense of satisfaction filled him. Let the games begin.

"Jacinda." Audrey Brummond took Jacey's hands in both of hers and kissed the air near her cheek. "What a wonderful surprise. You can't imagine how thrilled I was when Peter informed me that you'd be coming." She lowered her voice confidentially, her words oozing a sympathy that wasn't reflected in the avid look in her eyes. "How are you doing, dear?"

"I'm fine, Audrey. Busy, of course. You're looking well."

"You're sweet to say so. I didn't sleep at all last night. The details of this party preyed on my mind until dawn." The woman gave up her pretense of interest in the conversation and switched her attention to Lucky. "And who is your guest, Jacinda? I don't believe I've ever had the pleasure."

Before Jacey could open her mouth, Lucky took the

woman's hand in his, bent over it. "The pleasure is mine, Mrs. Brummond. I'm Luc Boucher. Lucky to my friends. Jacey and I are…business associates." He imbued the phrase with enough meaning to have the woman's look turning speculative.

"How…interesting. Have you two known each other long?"

Sensing that Jacey was about to respond, he inserted smoothly, "Years, actually." He sent an amused glance at the woman by his side. "Have you been keeping me a secret, *cher?*"

"Lucky and I—"

"—are parched." Lucky ignored Jacey's fuming gaze as he interrupted her. "I hope you'll excuse us while we get some refreshments."

"Of course, where are my manners?" Audrey waved a languid hand at a white-jacketed waiter. "There's champagne and wine on the serving trays, and a bar is set up on the terrace if you'd like something stronger."

With a hand at the base of Jacey's back, Lucky guided her away.

"We need to set some ground rules." Her lips were fixed in a smile, but her teeth were tightly clenched. "I do not want you giving the impression that we're…that is, that you and I are…"

"Lovers?" he supplied helpfully. "But why not? People will think what they want, and surely you'd prefer that they believe you've already replaced Peter than to think you hauled another man along for appearances only."

That seemed to silence her for a moment, and he took the time to scan the crowd that filled the large room. More people were on the terrace outside the open

French doors. He spotted Brummond surrounded by a group outside. As the waiter stopped before them, he took two glasses, and handed one to Jacey.

"I probably shouldn't drink," she said doubtfully. "I haven't had anything to eat since breakfast."

"Then we'll have to trip one of those maids carrying the hors d'oeuvre trays." He wasn't certain whether to be offended or amused at the faintly panicked look she threw him. "Relax, I'm on my best behavior tonight. Drink. Drink." He watched as she gulped from her glass with a faintly frantic air. Even if she got a bit tipsy, he didn't think that would harm anything. If anything, she'd do better if she relaxed a bit.

When her glass was half empty, he said, "Now. Tell me who you know here."

"Almost everyone." He wasn't sure how she could be certain, since he hadn't seen her give more than a quick glance around. "The Brummonds and my family have been friends for years. Peter and I grew up together."

"My sympathies. Turn your face toward mine."

"What?" Nervously, Jacey drained her glass before looking at Lucky. Somehow he seemed to be looming closer, but when she would have stepped back, his hand on her back prevented it. "So." He angled his face to gaze into her eyes in what, she was certain, would appear a loving fashion. Then he lifted his hand to brush a strand of hair back from her jaw, lingering there to caress the skin with the back of his knuckle. "Let me explain how we will play this."

Flames flickered to life beneath his touch. Or maybe she was heating up from the champagne. "Play what?"

"Our relationship tonight. We'll stay right here, appearin' engrossed in each other until someone approaches us. Given the fact that you know most people here, it's only a matter of time." Mindful of the press of bodies, he lowered his voice. "Our interest in each other won't go unnoticed. We won't have to offer explanations for our relationship, people will draw their own conclusions. That way you won't have to lie."

There was something wrong with his suggestion, but she couldn't think what it was. A rather pleasant haze had settled over her mind, filling her with a sense of well-being that she was still alert enough to recognize as false.

She sneaked a peek at the crowd beyond Lucky's shoulder. They'd already drawn attention, or rather, he had. More than one woman was staring at him with an avaricious gleam in her eye. And there were men watching them, too, their curiosity tinged with suspicion. Jacey couldn't blame them. Lucky looked like a very sleek, very lethal panther set down amidst a group of domestic housecats. That aura of danger would be its own kind of lure for some females, seeking to warm themselves by the inner fire he never quite managed to hide.

Her empty glass was taken from her hand, and his full one pressed into it. "Lucky, I don't need any more."

"*'Tite*, did I tell you how beautiful you look tonight?"

The endearment, accompanied by the warmth in his eyes, had her protest dying on her lips. His gaze was intense, momentarily fogging her senses. And in that instant, it wasn't difficult at all to understand his reputed success with women. It was only a wonder that more weren't tempted to trip him and wrestle him to the floor.

"Jacinda!" It was almost a relief to have her attention torn away from his heated gaze, even if it was to return a hug from the woman who'd been bearing down on them. Sluggishly, her brain kicked in, supplying her with a name. "Emily Jane, it's been a long time. I thought you were in Paris."

The brunette clad in a flame-red dress slit up to her thigh, made a casual gesture. "I was, then I got bored and came home. I'd heard you'd been hiding out, but now..." She drew back and looked Lucky over head to toe. "I can see why you've been otherwise occupied."

It took far more effort than it should have to resist from planting her spiked heel in the center of the woman's foot and grinding mercilessly. She was staring at Lucky like a well-fed feline peering at a saucer of cream.

"Emily Jane, this is Lucky Boucher, my...friend." Even to her own ears, the word seemed imbued with innuendo. She felt a sense of helplessness wash over her. Lucky had been right. People were going to draw their own conclusions. She just hadn't been prepared to be cast in the role of a sex-crazed seductress.

"Hello, *friend*," the other woman purred, as Lucky took her outstretched hand. "Jacinda has really been quite selfish to keep you all to herself like that. Not that I blame her."

Jacey held her breath, afraid his reaction would threaten the pretense they were creating. Lucky had never made any bones about his appreciation of women. Plural. And Emily Jane was making no secret of her interest.

So it was with mingled relief and pleasure that she heard him say, "I'm afraid I'm to blame for Jacey neglectin' her friends lately. We get so little time together, and I don't like to share." There was that light in his eyes again, the one that caught and held hers. He was really very, very good at this, she thought fuzzily. She moistened her lips, saw his gaze trace the movement. *Very good.*

"Jacinda, I'm so jealous, I just can't say. Would you mind getting me a martini, Mr. Boucher? Jacinda and I are going to talk about you while you're gone." Emily Jane sent him a coy look that filled Jacey with the irresistible urge to slap her. It wasn't as if she and Lucky were really a couple, but the other woman didn't know that, did she? She was all but lapping the man up.

"Of course." Lucky turned to Jacey. His midnight eyes were alight with amusement. "What can I get for you, darlin'?"

"I'm fine."

He gave a slow lazy smile in response and turned to wind his way outside to the portable bar, while Emily Jane squeezed Jacey's arm. "I'm sure you're better than fine with *friends* like that. Wherever did you find him?"

"We're…business associates."

Emily Jane blinked for a moment before throwing her head back and trilling out a laugh. "Oh, that's a new one. How delicious. And to think most of the busybodies here tonight were looking forward to seeing you show up, looking awkward and miserable." At Jacey's expression, she waved a hand. "Oh, you know it's true. But you've managed to create quite a different scene for yourself, haven't you?" From her tone it was apparent that she had been one of the ones looking forward to the first scenario she'd described. "Does Peter know?"

Peter. The sip of champagne Jacey was taking at the time went down wrong, and she sputtered out a cough. She thought, she was almost sure, she'd seen the man standing outside earlier, which meant that Lucky was likely to meet up with him.

"Excuse me, will you?" With little diplomacy she headed in the direction Lucky had taken. It would be best if the two of them stuck together. She absolutely didn't want him speaking to Peter unless she was there as a buffer.

Perhaps it was her imagination, but the crowd seemed to have grown thicker. And every few steps she took she was stopped by one guest after another, ostensibly wanting to say hello, but mostly pumping her for information about the man she'd come with. It seemed as though Lucky's plan had worked like a charm. She wished she could be certain that it wouldn't come back to haunt her.

It was a good fifteen minutes before she freed herself and got to the French door. A quick glance outside and she saw that Lucky was leaning against the bar, talking to Jarrett Carmichael, Emily's brother. Peter was nowhere in sight, and she breathed a little easier.

At least until she heard the voice at her elbow, which threatened to strangle the oxygen in her lungs. "Well played, dear."

Jacey swung around to find her mother at her side. Sotto voce, the woman continued, "Ever since I walked through the door, I've been bombarded with questions about you and your mystery man. I can't tell you how gratified I was to hear you'd taken my advice." She took Jacey's elbow in her hand and steered her toward a corner where they could speak uninterrupted. "Tell me, which of the men did you bring?"

Throwing a panicked gaze back outside, Jacey

shifted her weight, trying to block her mother's view of the terrace. "No one. I mean, I brought a friend of mine."

"Well, whoever it is seems to have done the trick." Satisfaction filled her mother's voice as she angled her head to look around the room. "Which one is he? Audrey Brummond was very nearly speechless from all accounts, and I must say, I would have paid to have seen…" Her words abruptly stopped and her expression froze. With a feeling of resignation, Jacey realized she'd spotted Lucky over her shoulder.

"I'm glad you approve," she said evenly. "I was far more comfortable bringing a friend than calling a stranger from your list. But you were right about not coming alone."

"Have you gone insane?" The deadly undertone was at odds with the pleasant look on Charlotte's face. Appearances, after all, were of the utmost importance. "How could you bring him here? He's totally unsuitable to work with, much less to let people believe you're involved with."

"On the contrary, my appearance with Lucky seems to have robbed the gossips of their fodder tonight." Jacey gave a defiant little shrug. "Now if you'll excuse me, Mother, I'm going to go rescue Lucky before those women out there perform a strip search on him."

She took advantage of her mother's momentary silence to slip outside. Fixing a bright smile on her face, she moved to Lucky's side. Or at least as close to his side as possible, considering the fact that he was two deep in women. Spying her, he murmured something and extricated himself with a finesse she would have admired if she'd been in the mood to appreciate it.

"Having a good time?"

He handed her a drink she didn't want and shrugged uncomfortably. "I'm thinkin' of asking for combat pay. You have some very…hungry acquaintances."

Making an attempt to avoid looking at the group of women who even now were gazing covetously at him, she raised the glass to her lips to hide her smirk. "I'll bet you thought these sorts of things were civilized."

"*Non.* But *subtle* would be an improvement."

"It's more like sophisticated warfare." Someone bumped her, and she stepped closer to him. "I suppose I should have warned you, though. Given you time to don a bulletproof vest or something."

He straightened with a jerk, and threw a narrowed glance at the redhead who'd brushed by him and was even now giving him a coy look. With one hand going to his backside, he muttered, "I don't think a vest would have provided me the protection where I most need it."

She snickered and tipped her glass to her lips again. A moment later she froze in the act. In the far corner of the terrace was stationed the happy couple. And from the expression on Peter's face, he'd not only spotted her, but recognized her companion.

Her good humor abruptly evaporated. "Toughen up, Boucher. The best part is yet to come. It's time to go over and congratulate Peter and his fiancée."

Ironically, that did seem to cheer Lucky up. He turned to follow the direction of her gaze, and a smile crossed his lips. He raised his glass in a mock toast toward the man who was still glaring at them, and then turned back to Jacey with a wicked light dancing in his eyes. "You know, I think you're right. And if I'm not mistaken, this just might be the highlight of the evenin'."

"Lucky," she said in a warning tone as they began moving in the direction of the two. "Behave yourself."

"Darlin'." His hand went to her bare back, for a quick heated caress before settling familiarly on the curve of her hip. "What fun would that be?"

She was saved from answering by the crush of people on all sides of them. They had joined a swell of well-wishers who were taking turns paying their regards to the couple. The wait didn't bother her. The man at her side did. He was firmly back into play-acting mode again, taking every occasion to touch her, lean close to whisper in her ear, and playing her lover with a dedication worthy of a Tony Award winner. So when she should have been spending the minutes thinking of something nonchalant and witty to say to Peter, she was constantly being distracted by the weight of Lucky's hand at her waist, the tingle of awareness that trailed after he touched her arm, her shoulder, her throat.

"This is not helping," she breathed into his ear, catching his hand before it roamed to her bottom. More than once she'd seen Peter's gaze on them, and his countenance had gone stony.

"You don't think?" He gave her a slow smile accompanied by a lazy wink. Reaching out, he toyed with a strand of her hair, wrapping the end around his index finger. "Me, I think it's brilliant."

Her response went unuttered. The people in front of them parted and suddenly they were faced with Peter Brummond and his fiancée. A tension-filled second ticked by. Another. Then a lifetime of Charlotte's drilling on etiquette clicked in and Jacey smiled warmly, held out her hand to the woman. "Hello, I'm Jacinda Wheeler. Peter's family and mine are old friends." Far from the timid woman described by Brummond, Longwaite seemed amply able to hold her own in any given situation. She shook Jacey's hand briefly before slipping a proprietary arm through Peter's.

Brummond smiled thinly. "Celeste, darling, you remember me mentioning Jacinda."

"Of course I do."

So she'd warranted a mention? Jacey entertained a very brief, very satisfying mental image of him wearing the remainder of her drink. She turned to smile at the man by her side. "And this is Luc Boucher, a friend of mine."

Lucky took Celeste's hand in both of his. "Brummond is a lucky man. I hope you remind him of that often."

Jacey managed, barely, to avoid rolling her eyes as the petite woman simpered. "How kind of you to say so. Are you and Jacinda…close?"

The look he turned on Jacey then was heated enough to steal her breath. "Quite close."

It took conscious effort to tear her gaze away, to remember to draw air into her lungs again. Smiling even more brightly, she stepped forward and brushed a kiss on Peter's cheek. "Congratulations." Turning to Celeste, she said graciously, "I wish you both every happiness. But we really shouldn't keep you from the rest of your guests any longer. Lucky?"

She had the distant thought that she'd always detested the way Peter pressed his lips into a thin flat line when he was displeased. That, and the muscle twitching in his jaw was enough to fill her with a flicker of satisfaction. Whatever the fallout from the little charade she and Lucky had enacted here tonight, it had accomplished one thing. She'd walk out of this event with her head held high.

They were some distance away before she remembered to draw a breath. "Well, that was fun." She sipped from her glass again, frowned when she found it empty.

"I thought so. She'll lead him around by the nose. Already has a pretty firm hook there, I'd say."

"Then he's getting exactly what he deserves." And she wasn't going to waste a moment of sympathy on him. Delicate colored lanterns had been hung to light the grounds near the terrace. They followed a stone walk along the gardens, edging farther away from the sounds of the party. The evening had turned out far better than she had hoped, Jacey thought. If she'd come alone, the entire night would have been excruciating. And if she'd followed her mother's advice, it would have been humiliating, as well.

Thoughts of her mother sliced into her sense of well-being. "I should probably warn you that Charlotte is here, and she is not happy."

"Such a surprise, for the woman is usually a fount of good cheer."

His incredulous tone brought an unwilling smile to her lips. "You do seem to bring out a rather…sour side in her. She was thrilled that I'd brought a companion, until she saw who it was."

He gave a casual shrug. "I have long been convinced that you were adopted. That one is much too cold to have gotten a child in the usual way."

She elbowed him in the ribs. "Don't be nasty. I'm feeling much too good to argue with you."

"Then don't. Dance with me instead."

"Dance?"

He cocked his head. "The band is startin'. Don't you hear it?"

Orchestral strains drifted over the air. She turned back toward the terrace and saw a few couples already swaying to the music. "I suppose it would help the cause if we stayed around a bit longer."

He offered his bent arm. "I aim to please. Let's give them just a little more to talk about, shall we?"

Resting her hand on his arm, she smiled brilliantly up at him. "Let's."

Never, in the furthest reach of her imagination, had Jacey ever considered she'd actually enjoy herself tonight. But for the remainder of the evening, she did exactly that. Lucky was an amazingly good dancer, although he held her much closer than she was really comfortable with. But it was difficult to protest when she saw the sidelong glances sent their way, and knew that regardless of the impression he was planting, no one in the place was feeling sorry for Jacinda Wheeler.

Because he insisted, they nibbled at hors d'oeuvres before he'd bring her another drink, and then they danced again. She thought it was safe enough to remain on the terrace, as her mother rarely joined in the dancing.

She had just a flicker of conscience when someone mentioned to her in passing that Charlotte had left early with a headache, knowing just what, or who, had generated it. But it wasn't all that difficult to banish the thought from her mind. She didn't fool herself into thinking that she'd heard the end of this from her mother. It was much more likely that the woman had retreated for the moment to fortify a new attack. But she wasn't going to worry about that at the moment. She was enjoying herself too much.

An hour later she excused herself to find the rest room. With a backwards glance she saw that Lucky was immediately claimed by Peter's seventy-year-old great-aunt. With a smile on her face, she wound her way through the living room and out to the hallway. It shouldn't surprise her that women of all ages responded to the man. The charisma he exuded transcended generations.

"Jacinda."

Lost in her thoughts, she started a bit at the voice coming from behind her. Turning, her good mood abruptly splintered. "Peter." Looking beyond him, she inquired, "Where's your fiancée?"

"Dancing with my father. Can we talk for a bit?" It was really more of a command than a request, accompanied as it was by his hand on her back, guiding her into the study. But it was the cautious look he threw up and down the hallway before closing the door that had the bubbles of temper firing through her veins.

"Really, Peter, do you think this is wise?"

He turned to face her. "That was almost exactly what I was going to ask you. What the hell is going on between you and Boucher?"

The demand, the anger behind it, stunned her for a moment. When she could manage to form an answer, she responded spiritedly, "What possible business is that of yours?"

He had the grace to flush. "Things didn't work out between us, Jacinda, but I still care what happens to you. By playing games with Boucher, you're going to wind up getting hurt."

"That isn't possible."

Her dismissal of his words made him more irate. "Dammit, give me some credit. I know you, and I'm all too familiar with men like him. I never did understand why you hired him."

She wandered about the room, running one hand over the butter-soft leather furniture. "He's good at his job, Peter. He's good…at a great many things." The words shocked her even as they left her lips. But they seemed to infuriate the man standing before her.

"Were you carrying on with him behind my back?"

The sheer audacity of the words surprised a laugh from her. Belatedly, her sense of the ridiculous kicked in. "You used to have a fine appreciation of irony. Surely you can see just how ludicrous that question is, coming from you."

"All right, I behaved badly. I should have ended our relationship when I started seeing Celeste, but we have a history…our families have a connection…" He made a gesture with his hand. "What do you want from me? Things happened quickly, and I had to do the gentlemanly thing, to avoid talk. It hasn't been easy for me, either, Jacinda."

She stared at him, struggling to piece together what he was saying. He'd been seeing Celeste while the two of them were still dating? The spike of anger that accompanied the realization was sidetracked as the rest of his words filtered in. "Gentlemanly? Celeste is pregnant?" His pursed lips, his gaze skirting hers, was her answer. "Well. You were busy."

"The situation was impossible," he muttered, half turning away. "We've waited this long to announce our engagement to quell the gossip."

There was a dangerous burn in her stomach. She decided he was far safer with the furniture between them. "I suppose I should be grateful. No woman likes it to become common knowledge that her boyfriend of a year and a half knocked up another woman while they were still dating."

"We're having a private ceremony, and then I'll transfer to father's Houston branch for a couple of years. No one will ever put the timeline together, you can be sure."

She shook her head, incredulous. The lengths he was taking were reminiscent of a generation earlier. With a sudden dawn of understanding, she realized the truth. "I'm sure Audrey will be pleased that you're following her plans so exactly."

His voice was stiff. "I don't blame Mother for her concerns. Both your family and mine have always been careful about their reputations. Which is one more reason you should take greater care with yours."

For a moment, she'd actually begun to feel a bit sorry for him. The sensation dissipated as he went on. "He's only interested in one thing from you, Jacinda. You have to protect yourself."

Her smile was brittle. "Believe me, I know exactly where Lucky's interests lie."

He gave her a pitying look. "He may be using sex to get close to you, but make no mistake, it's your money he's after." He didn't appear to notice that she'd gone completely, deadly still. "A man of his sort doesn't choose a woman like you for a relationship without ulterior motives."

Tiny glaciers formed, bumping and colliding in her veins. "A woman like me?"

Her frigid tone seemed lost on him. But then, Peter always had been singularly dense at times. Not to mention insufferably insensitive. "Like is attracted to like. A lowlife like Boucher has certain…appetites. You don't have the experience or skill to satisfy a man like that, unless it's with your bank account. So just be careful, will you?"

The buzzing in her ears had nothing to do with the alcohol she'd imbibed and everything to do with fury. Hot molten waves of it, whipping through her body, licking along nerve endings. Outside her defense courses she'd never hit a person in her life, but she wanted, with every fiber of her being, to ball her fist and plant it squarely in the nose his plastic surgeon had so carefully structured when he'd been eighteen.

It took every bit of acting ability she possessed to smile sweetly. "I'll keep it in mind. But you should keep in mind that my…skill, as you call it, hasn't been an issue with Lucky. So maybe it's not the type of woman that matters at all. Maybe it's the type of man."

And with that she turned on her heel and walked regally from the room.

Chapter 6

"The nerve of that slimy rat."

Lucky watched with mild concern as Jacey paced the length of her parlor. Wearing heels the height of hers, it wouldn't take much to catch her foot on the richly jeweled tapestry rug, or to twist an ankle when she turned, skirt fluttering intriguingly around her slender legs, to pace back again. He didn't consider his concern diluted at all for being layered with appreciation. He'd never denied being male.

"*My* skill. *My* experience. Can you believe that? Like he was anything spectacular in that department."

"The man's a fool." He poured some wine he'd opened in the hopes of calming her, and pressed a glass into her hand. She drank it with a speed that showed little sensitivity for its label. With a shrug, he refilled her glass as she passed by again. "It's the sort of thing a small man says to tear at a woman's ego. If he'd had any particular skill at all, he would have had no complaints about yours."

"Exactly." She whirled to survey him grimly. "And I told him as much, too. Well, actually, I let him believe that you had reason to know it wasn't the truth, but after the show you put on tonight, I didn't think you'd mind."

His lips quirked. "*Non,* use me as you will." He watched, with growing worry, as she tossed back the contents of the glass and handed it to him. They hadn't eaten tonight other than the fancy snacks that had been served at the party, and he hadn't noted that Jacey had eaten all that much then. "Maybe you could just hook the bottle to an IV."

She stood before him, one hip jutted out, chin raised and gaze narrowed. "I don't need a lecture, Lucky, I have my mother for that."

Given his opinion of Charlotte Wheeler, it was a low blow, but effective. He shut up. By the time she realized he was right, she'd be nursing the grandmother of all headaches.

Right now, though, she was on a roll. He settled on the curved-back couch to enjoy the sight she made with color in her cheeks and fire in her eyes. He'd always had a fine appreciation for a woman in a temper. *Bien sûr,* it usually did not pay to underestimate the danger of a female in such a state. But in this case, he wasn't the cause of the fury so he thought himself safe enough.

"I could kneecap him for you." He tossed out the offer lazily, only half joking. "I doubt he'd put up much of a fight, and I can't say that the urge has never occurred."

She slowed as she crossed the room yet again, her

lips tilted. "The idea has merit, but I think I'd find it more gratifying if I did it myself."

"Very possibly. I will settle, in that case, for a ring-side seat."

"He got her pregnant, did I tell you that?" There was a flash of emotion in her eyes that had all amusement draining from him in an instant. "He was sleeping with both of us at the same time. From the haste with which they're marrying, I wouldn't be surprised if we were still seeing each other when that blessed event occurred."

"Maybe I'll rethink that kneecap job, after all." As it was, Brummond would be fortunate if their paths didn't cross anytime soon. He no longer questioned just where this protective streak toward Jacey stemmed from. He could consider her well rid of the man while still want-ing to break his jaw.

. She gave a wave of her hand, as if it didn't matter. But he could see the disillusionment under her anger. "He was just so smug, so sure of himself when he said you could only be interested in me for money. I wanted to strangle him."

He got up to pour himself some wine. It looked like it was going to be a long night. "My philosophy has al-ways been, don't get mad, get even." He gazed at her over the rim of his glass. "You could always start sleepin' around. When he hears glowin' reports of your aptitude, he'd go insane with jealousy."

To his amazement, she seemed to take his jest seri-ously. "But I can't, don't you see? Because there's a part of me that wonders if he was right, damn him." She stared broodingly into her wine. "I haven't exactly had a legion of lovers. If I'd had, I could laugh in his face, knowing the lack of passion I felt was due to him, not me. But...I don't know that. And since I can't be certain, I don't dare get involved with anyone else, because then he'll find out I'm terrible in bed, too. And if I don't ever have any other lovers, there's no way to get more experience so that I gain more confidence. It's really a catch-22."

Because his jaw had dropped during the course of that astonishing revelation, he took pains to close it. But he was unable to remain silent for long. "Jacey, if you still lack experience after being in his bed, Brummond is the incompetent, not you."

"You're just being polite."

"I have horrible manners, remember? You're always remindin' me."

"Still." She looked pensive. "You're hardly in the position to judge, since we've never slept together. And it's really not exactly the sort of thing I can ask my former lovers, now, is it?"

Even without her earlier words, he'd have bet that the list of her former lovers would be a short one. He sneaked a look at the half-empty wine bottle. He would never have guessed that too much wine on an empty stomach would loosen Jacey's tongue to this extent, but he couldn't say he minded the phenomenon. She was displaying more real emotion in this state than she normally let herself show in a week. And in doing so, she was utterly beguiling.

He wasn't certain how to erase the doubt from her expression. How could someone who looked like she did be so unaware of her own appeal? It was a mystery of nature, but then, women were mysterious creatures.

If it had been anyone else, he could have pulled her into his arms and shown her just how much woman she was, but this wasn't just any woman. It was Jacey.

There hadn't been a man at the party tonight who hadn't taken a second and third look at her in that dress. With her hair loose and a little tangled—an improvement of his own design—she'd looked far more approachable than usual. Even more tempting. The contrast between her appearance and her usual reserved manner couldn't help but send a man's imagination into overdrive.

She came over and sat down next to him on the couch with a little sigh. "Leave it to Peter to ruin what had actually turned out to be an enjoyable evening. He always was a fun-hater."

The term had him chuckling. "Somehow I don't find that surprisin'. And knowin' what you do about him, you should realize he only said what he did to make you miserable."

"I wish I could believe that. As pompous and supercilious as he was, he was also quite sincere." She frowned, as if she were puzzling over some aspect of a particularly confusing case.

"He was jealous, *cher*. He doesn't want you, but he doesn't want you to be happy either. Not really." He picked up her hand, kissed it lightly, then laid it back on her lap. "Trust me, I know these things. Unlike you, I do not lack experience." That last was uttered with a wicked tone designed to get a rise out of her.

"So I've gathered." Her gaze slid to his, and he didn't trust the speculative gleam in them. "Maybe you *can* help me, after all."

"Anything. As I've proven tonight, I'm at your service."

She smiled, slow and satisfied and he had the distinct impression that he'd stepped neatly into a trap. "That's just where I want you. At my service, so to speak."

He choked, spewing wine down his shirt front. She couldn't possibly have meant that the way it had sounded. "Careful. A less astute man would have assumed you meant…"

"That I want to sleep with you? That is what I meant."

His throat seemed to have closed completely. His lungs shut down. But the rest of his body was showing remarkable signs of interest.

"It'd be the perfect solution, don't you see?" She turned to face him on the couch, her expression earnest. "If even a fraction of what I've heard of your reputation is true, I'm bound to pick up some skills during our time together. There's no worry about sticky entanglements, because when it's over we'd still be friends. It's really the perfect setup."

Perfectly crazy. "You have to be kiddin'." He peered more closely at her. Was she tipsier than he'd realized?

"Why? We're friends, aren't we? Friends help each other."

He was beginning to feel hunted. And tempted. *Mon Dieu,* was he tempted. What man wouldn't be? He'd never been overburdened with much of a conscience, but he had enough to know he'd never forgive himself if he agreed to her outrageous suggestion.

She tilted her head, and he caught a hint of her perfume, something light and elusive that was meant to leave a man wanting to get closer. He straightened, putting a measure of distance between them. Getting closer was the last thing he should be considering right now.

"If I'd known it only took a little wine to get you to this point, I'd have been plyin' you with it the first day we met." As a joke, it failed miserably. Her expression didn't lighten, nor did she look away.

"If you've been wanting to since the day we met, why should you be having second thoughts now that the opportunity has presented itself?"

She made a good argument, he admitted to himself. It was that damn logical mind of hers. There wasn't a thing he was going to say that wouldn't dig his hole a little deeper. Still, he had to try.

"It isn't a good idea for friends to get involved."

"So you prefer to go to bed with people you don't like? Really?" Her tone was surprised.

"*Oui.* I mean, no." It was hard to stay focused when she was gazing at him so intently, her blue eyes seeming darker, deeper, than he'd remembered. "What I meant was, sex is easy with people you can walk away from after the relationship is over. It gets complicated to move a friendship to an intimate level, and then back again."

"But that's all in the expectations, isn't it? I could see the problem if one of the parties decided they wanted more, but you and I already know what we want—to go back to being friends after it's over." She shook her head. "I can't believe you're making this so difficult. You of all people should be able to handle this."

His temper began to simmer, ignited by a tide of frustration. "Why me of all people? Because I'm just a bum who uses women and tosses them aside when another one comes along?" He uttered the words like a dare, waiting for her to agree. There was just enough truth in the words for them to sting. But to hear that she believed the same would lash unmercifully.

"Of course not." She was regarding him cautiously. "I'm just pointing out that you should have a great deal of experience in ending things neatly. I trust you, Lucky. Call me crazy, but I do. I'd never suggest such a thing to anyone else." She gave a self-deprecating laugh. "I'd never discuss such a thing with anyone else."

He felt like a cartoon character with a little red-horned devil on one shoulder and an angel on the other, each offering conflicting advice. He was much more used to listening to the demon. Just the thought of taking Jacey to bed, of undressing her leisurely, of discovering all the secret sacred places where her scent lingered was more temptation than one man should have to bear. He'd never been one to avoid temptation. What was the point, when giving in to it was so much more pleasurable?

It was as if a door he'd thought safely locked had been wedged open, summoning every wicked thought he'd been firmly suppressing since they'd met. Once he'd made the conscious decision to stay with the job he'd finagled from her, he'd had to lay some ground rules for himself. It didn't take an expert to realize that sex and business didn't mix.

She was leaning toward him, just a little, and the neckline of her dress gaped, just enough to reveal the curve of her breast above its lacy cup. Abruptly he lost his train of thought. Her skin would be sleek as stroked silk, warm and inviting to the touch. And he wanted to touch. Too much.

His conscience was getting harder to hear. It never had had a very loud speaking voice. It was easier to focus on the long line of her throat, on the pulse beating at its base. Really, what was the harm? They could both handle this. It could work, couldn't it, if both of them wanted it to?

Somehow her mouth seemed nearer. Had she moved, or had he? He was positive he hadn't. Almost completely certain. Without conscious thought he reached up and laid his index finger against that pulse, felt each tiny beat. A woman's body had a myriad of places where the pulse would pound just that strong, just that wild. For an instant he allowed himself to imagine what it would be like to be able to discover all of them for himself.

Her eyelids drooped invitingly. Her lips parted. It would be so easy to close the distance between them, to see if her lips were as soft as they looked. To shape them with his own and for just a moment discover their taste, their texture.

Three years ago he would never have hesitated. There was no shame in taking what a woman freely offered. But that was then, and those other women were different. They weren't Jacey.

He could feel her breath on his lips, the sweetness its own kind of enticement. What was the harm of one kiss, after all? It might be just the thing to bring her to her senses. *Oui,* she would be so shocked about crossing this line that she would see her suggestion for what it was. A foolish idea. His lips brushed hers, whisper-soft. Insane even.

Insanity had never been so exhilarating.

He returned for another taste, and then another. And

then all thought receded as he turned more fully toward her, slid his hand into her hair and angled his mouth more completely over hers. With an eagerness he would have denied, he pressed her lips open and swept his tongue into her mouth.

Her flavor was heady and somehow familiar, although he'd never kissed her before. But he'd thought of it. Years ago, before he'd known that this woman would come to mean more to him than he'd ever believed possible, he'd spent long, sleepless nights lying in bed staring up at the cracked water-stained ceiling in his apartment, considering doing exactly this, and more.

She gave a little gasp, and he swallowed the small sound, scored her bottom lip with his teeth. It was just a kiss, meant to be savored and enjoyed. When it was over he didn't want to be left with any regrets. It would be a shame to let the opportunity pass and still be plagued with questions about her response, the exquisite softness of her lips or the precise pressure it took to elicit the greatest pleasure.

And for a moment he thought it was going to be just that easy, a kiss between two friends, a casual exchange that would put to rest the clamoring that had long been under his skin. Then her tongue met his in a long velvet glide, and the muscles in his belly clenched. The angle of the kiss changed, became deeper, hotter. There was heat here, the kind that could torch control and sear nerve endings. That warning whispered across his mind, was banished. He wasn't a man to lose his head over a mere kiss.

Her fingers threaded into his hair, pressing him closer and he willingly complied. Her mouth ate at his, hungry and demanding, making a mockery of restraint.

Jacey could feel little licks of flame lapping up her spine, a conflagration of the senses. She'd known he'd be good at this. Expert, even. What she hadn't reckoned on was her own reaction. There was something about the taste of him, something a little wild and untamed. The primitive responses that lurked in all men were just a bit closer to the surface with him. There would be no holding back with Lucky; he'd be the type of man to demand everything she had to offer, and more. The realization should have frightened her. It only fanned the flames higher.

She fumbled with the buttons on his shirt, wanting to feel sleek warm skin beneath her fingertips. Slipping one hand inside, she flexed her fingers, nearly purring at the warmth that transferred from the taut muscles there to her palm. Sex held no secrets for her; she wasn't a virgin. But somehow she knew that intimacy with this man would shatter any previous experience she'd ever had.

He pressed her back until her shoulders were against the arm of the sofa. She pulled him with her, wanting to prolong the contact. She needn't have worried. He followed her down, fitting himself closely against her.

Lucky dragged his lips away from hers to investigate the curve of her jaw, the long column of her throat. The pulse at its base scrambled madly, each tiny beat an invitation. He flicked the tip of his tongue across it, then was sidetracked by the trail of fragrance that traced from that spot to the sweet soft place beneath her ear. He hadn't reckoned on this, that one taste of her would be enough to dim reason, haze judgment. He'd never been a man to be controlled by his impulses, but he couldn't deny that the immediate attraction he'd felt for her all that time ago had only been tucked away, not extinguished. It had burst forth full-strength as soon as he'd touched her, like a flood from a crumbling dike.

His mouth returned to hers, hunger whipping through his veins. He wanted more. He wanted to strip the dress from her, delighting in the freedom to kiss and caress every inch of that velvety skin. Every brush of her fingers on his chest notched his temperature up a bit higher.

He smoothed a hand along her curves, the slender thigh, the rounded hip, the indentation of her waist. The journey was both enticing and frustrating. He didn't want to feel the fabric between them, nor silk and lace. He wanted, more than was comfortable, to have her naked and take her with all the passion he'd been setting aside for years.

There was a hint of roughness in the pressure of his mouth, but Jacey welcomed it. A simple kiss had never elicited this depth of emotion in her before, but then, there was nothing simple about this. Teeth clashed, tongues battled in a sensual struggle that held more than a tinge of impatience.

She pushed the jacket off his shoulders, down his arms. He had to shed it to avoid being shackled. She used the opportunity to tug his shirt from his pants and release the rest of the buttons, then smoothed her hands over his torso.

He muttered a curse against her neck and she smiled a little, satisfied. Despite all his earlier arguments, he couldn't deny a response. They were pressed too closely together for her to be unaware of his reaction to her. It fueled her own, burned through her usual reserve to reach out and take exactly what she wanted.

His chest was covered by a light patterning of black hair, and she stroked him, enjoying the feel of taut muscles beneath smooth skin. There wasn't an ounce of softness to be found. All angles and planes, with the most intriguing hollows left where bone met sinew. The lean toughness of his body wasn't a surprise, but her reaction to it was.

She wanted, quite desperately, to test the skin over his collarbone with teeth and tongue, to explore the softness of the hair beneath his arms, to knead his taut biceps and to feel his arms tightly around her, with nothing between them. The thoughts were foreign, yet strong enough to incite her to act; her intentions were all but shredded in the next instant.

Lucky swept his hand up her thigh, enjoying the texture of silk-encased satin. And then his fingers moved higher, and thought was shattered when he met a lacy nylon top with warm bare skin above it. His blood began to pound, hammering him from the inside out. He could feel the whisper of muscle beneath the silky softness, and was tortured by the knowledge that an even more exquisite softness was just inches away.

He stilled, breath torn raggedly from his lungs, as he waged a silent inner war. Opening his eyes, he tried to focus, nearly groaned when he did. The shoulder of her dress had slid down one shoulder, revealing the lacy strap of her bra, the curve of her breast. Around her shoulders her hair was a sexy tangle from his hands, and her lips were slightly parted and swollen from his kisses.

He'd never considered himself a particularly honorable man. Tough choices had always been more comfortable to skirt completely than to grapple with. But right here, right now, he waged the battle of his life, and whatever the outcome, he knew he'd be the loser.

She wasn't for him. He'd recognized that the first time he'd seen her, felt that first punch of desire. That fact had been hammered home again and again over the years. They were separated by background, bloodline and experience. He'd made his peace with that truth, and no one had been more surprised than he when they'd become friends despite it.

Her eyelids fluttered open, and the sheen of longing in her eyes nearly tipped the scales. They were dazed with lust, longing and something else, something he perhaps imagined but that threatened to unman him, nevertheless. Trust.

Wrenching himself away from her, he sat on the edge of the couch, forced oxygen into his lungs with great rasping breaths. His fists were clenched, as frustration and unchecked desire crashed and churned within him. He didn't have a chivalrous bone in his body, so there was no reason for this gallantry. No reason not to give into the passion they both felt, the edgy violent need that even now was clawing at him.

No reason but one.

"Lucky." Her voice, slightly slurred, held a question he didn't think he could answer. To keep his hands from reaching for her again, he busied them with buttoning his shirt.

"Take three aspirin and a couple glasses of water before you go to…sleep." Not bed. He definitely didn't want to think about her in bed. Alone. "It will lessen the effects of the alcohol."

There was a long silence, but as he reached for his

jacket, she straightened, swung her feet off the couch. It was only then that he saw she still wore the spike heels, and the realization scalded his senses all over again. For a brief self-indulgent moment he harbored a mental image of her bare, save for those shoes, thigh-high nylons and the scraps of lace she wore beneath her dress. Sweat beaded on his brow, and he tore his gaze away, bolting from the couch.

"I take it I'm going to be sleeping alone."

"*'Tite,* you could tempt a saint." Which he wasn't. Not by a long shot. "But tomorrow you'll be damn glad one of us stopped before it was too late."

"And if I'm not?"

Her soft question had him freezing in the act of shrugging into his jacket. What if time and sobriety had no effect on her decision? What then? Would he be able to withstand the temptation if she offered day after day?

His throat nearly closed at the thought. "You will be." He rose, strode to the door, and then paused, chanced one more glance at her. She was staring at him with wide, serious eyes, and that hint of vulnerability was back on her face. Jaw tightening, he looked away. "Lock the door after I leave. I'll see you tomorrow."

He didn't wait to hear her response before letting himself outside, welcoming the slap of cool air against his fevered skin. Jogging down the steps, he knew it was useless to go home. There would be no sleep for him right now. Maybe not for a long time.

So instead of returning to his apartment he cruised the interstate around the city. He lowered all the windows, wishing the rush of fall air would chase the heat from his veins. But as the hours of aimless driving passed, his gas tank showed signs of depletion, but his blood hadn't even begun to cool.

It had been a mistake to touch her. He'd known it even at the time. It had been reckless and supremely arrogant to believe that he could do so, even for a moment, and then walk away without repercussions. He'd been a *couillon* to even consider it. Tomorrow she'd be embarrassed by what had transpired, ill-at-ease with him. While he…he'd be haunted by her scent, her taste and the softness of her skin.

He had the dismal feeling that once opened, the door he'd locked against all those emotions wasn't going to be easily secured again.

It was hours before he returned to his apartment on Bienville Street. The business it was located above had first been a bar, then a strip club and currently housed a down-on-her-luck palm reader who ran a voodoo shop for gullible tourists. The psychic was the quietest neighbor he'd had so far. Although it was probably the sixth place he'd lived in since leaving the bayou, the apartment was almost interchangeable with his previous ones, down to the cracked plaster and water-stained ceilings.

Since he only slept there, it didn't make much sense to spend any real money on a place to live.

Lucky let himself into the apartment, then closed and locked the door behind him. Slipping off his jacket, he crossed to the bedroom and emptied the pockets onto the bedside table before hanging the jacket in the boxy closet.

He stripped, padded to the bathroom and stepped into the shower. Turning the water to a frigid, punishing spray, he swiped back his hair and lifted his face to it, welcoming the gradual cooling of his skin, if not his insides. Long minutes later he turned the faucet off, grabbed a towel and dried off carelessly, slicking his hair back with his fingers.

The process of readying for bed did nothing to summon sleep. He was still wired, but it was late, only a couple of hours from dawn. Walking into the bedroom, he switched on the lamp beside the bed and picked up the cell phone he'd set there earlier. Flipping through the options, he noted that he had three voice messages.

He pulled back the covers, slid into bed, pressed the key to replay them. The first was from Remy, and it was good to hear his friend's familiar voice in the near darkness.

"Lucky, where y'at? Gettin' it on with some hottie, prob'ly. Listen, Tante…she's…she's not good, *mon ami.* Not good at all."

His earlier feeling dissipated into concern. He could easily read the underlying emotion in the man's voice.

"She's dyin'. Tha's what they tell me. Can you believe that? Strongest damn woman you or I ever knew, right? 'Member when she caught us drinkin' that moonshine in back of the church and near about tore the hide off both of us?"

The memory summoned a smile and Lucky stared into the shadows, remembering the scene. They'd been thirteen, and both had given the woman more than a grudging respect ever since for the attempt, if not for her limited success. They'd both been damn fast, even then.

The message abruptly stopped. He must have run out of time. Lucky flipped to the next one and heard his friend's voice resume.

"I have to stay. I already called Vinny and let him know I wouldn't be back. I want to be with her now, for as long as I can. You can reach me at this number." He rattled one off. "It's cousine Lucille's house. She's bringing Tante here until..." There was an emotion-filled pause. "I'll call you—"

The message cut off again. Heart heavy, Lucky pressed the key to hear the third one, fully expecting to hear his friend again. Instead, he heard the unmistakable cultured tones that never failed to turn his veins to ice.

"Mr. Boucher. I don't know what game you think you're playing with my daughter, but rest assured it won't be tolerated." The tone would have been familiar even if the words hadn't given away the identity of the caller. Duchess to peasant, as if it pained her to even acknowledge his existence. It usually didn't bother him, knowing as he did that he had the upper hand in their encounters. But tonight he was feeling a bit too raw to summon his usual tolerance.

"I have a proposition for you, one I think you'll find attractive. Meet me at the Century Restaurant on Canal Street at 1:00 p.m. Monday. It would be in your best interests to keep this conversation from Jacinda. But as you seem to be quite adept at duplicity, I'm certain that won't be a problem for you."

He deleted the last message, taking some small pleasure at the thought of erasing the woman's voice. If only it were as easy to eliminate her from his memory. It was too easy to recall the first time he'd ever met her. That encounter had changed the course of his life in a way he could never have foreseen.

Deliberately, he sidestepped the recollections that

threatened to flood him. Shutting off the small lamp on the table next to the bed, he welcomed the engulfing shadows. Darkness could surround a man, dragging him under its shroud with no hope of ever seeing the light again. But it was guilt that could do the most damage.

Guilt could eat a man alive.

Chapter 7

Jacey looked up as her inner office door pushed open, her eyes widening slightly when she got a look at the man filling it. Glancing pointedly at her watch, she said, "Nice that you could make it, and before noon, too."

"Don't even start," Lucky warned, stalking in and helping himself to the carafe of coffee on the table. "I haven't had much sleep this weekend."

There was a stab of something that felt suspiciously like jealousy directly beneath her heart. She could only imagine what had kept him up last night, and the mental images weren't exactly a balm to her bruised feelings.

She'd both dreaded and anticipated this meeting. A part of her still squirmed at the blatant invitation she'd issued, which had been, eventually, turned down. She'd spent many long hours yesterday nursing a pounding head and a battered ego, until the hangover-induced haze had lifted, leaving her thoughts clear. And since every instant of the scene between them at her house was branded on her memory, she could recall the one thing that saved her from complete and utter humiliation: Lucky had wanted her. Maybe she'd forced the issue, but once he'd started kissing her, he hadn't wished to stop any more than she had.

She surveyed him again, a quick glance from under her lashes. He had his eyes closed, and he was drinking the coffee as if the caffeine provided a lifeline. Come to think of it, he didn't look like he normally did after he'd spent the night with one of his women. He wasn't teasing and smiling, and he lacked the loose-limbed grace he usually moved with. Right now he seemed as tightly wound as a clock, and there was no trace of a grin on his unshaven face.

Tapping her gold pen lightly against her desk, a tiny flame of hope flickered to life within her. It was a long shot, but what if his lack of sleep had been caused by *her?* By what had almost happened between them? Satisfaction stirred at the thought, tempered by uncertainty. Lucky wasn't like other men, and she didn't have the experience to do more than guess at what had caused his foul mood.

He lowered the cup, caught her staring at him. "What?" he snapped.

She arched her brows. "Nothing. I was just admiring your sunny disposition."

He eyed her suspiciously, but she kept her expression carefully bland. "I had some bad news this weekend."

Sympathy immediately rose. "I'm sorry. Your family?"

"*Non.* My friend's aunt. He and I grew up together."

He filled his coffee cup again, drank more slowly. "I drove home to visit them both yesterday and got back late last night."

The flicker of hope she'd nurtured for a moment was immediately doused. "Do you need some time off? Because I can handle the Garvey case alone until you get back, and everything else we have can wait for a while."

He shook his head. "I just wanted to pay my respects before Remy's *tante* died." And even more, he'd wanted to be at his friend's side for support if nothing else, while he was grappling with the inevitable. The situation had been sobering enough to have him swinging by his *grand-mère*'s house despite the late hour, as if to reassure himself of her continued good health.

Rounding the table, he propped his hips against it and studied her. If she'd had any ill effects from drinking too much the other night, it didn't show. She'd left her hair loose for once, to swirl around her shoulders in a sleek bell. Although he much preferred it the way it had been Saturday night, slightly mussed and tangled by his fingers, it looked good.

His gaze swept down her figure. She'd slipped off her matching jacket and the silky white shirt she wore beneath plainly showed the undergarment worn beneath. He searched his memory. A camisole, that's what it was. And the neckline of the blouse was softly V'd, instead of the buttoned-up nun attire she usually favored for work.

Then his eyes narrowed. If it had been anyone else, he would have wondered if the change was for his benefit. Surely not. Jacey wasn't the type for those kinds of games. He'd thought about how to play this all the way to the bayou and back. She'd be embarrassed, he'd decided. Probably find it difficult to face him. He'd been determined to make it a bit easier for her by playing it casual.

But she didn't look embarrassed. She looked… amused. And that fact did nothing to make him want to go easy on her. Dammit, she'd been the cause of his sleepless nights. And he sure couldn't see that she'd suffered any ill effects herself.

"How was the hangover?" he asked bluntly.

"Annoying. And don't gloat, it's unattractive."

He folded his arms across his chest. "Me? I'm not gloatin'. This is concern you see on my face." He paused a moment. "Although I distinctly remember tellin' you to go easy on the wine once we got to your place."

"You said a lot of things…once we got to my place."

He had the distinct feeling he was about to step in quicksand. Sidestepping it nimbly, he nodded to the papers on her desk. "Is that the Garvey file? How do you want to split up the family members?"

"I have some feelers out with a friend of mine at the FTC to see if I can get the scoop on the case they were building against Stephen. Until that information comes through, I'll focus on Mark. You can take Amanda." She reached for one of the file folders on her desk, and handed it to him. "I've listed the names and addresses of her ex-husbands. All of them live in the state. You might want to start with them. It shouldn't be too difficult to get copies of the divorce decrees from each. I'd be very interested in finding out if she's paying alimony to any of them." Since the proceedings would be a matter of public record, they'd be available through the courthouse database.

"I don't feel like sittin' at a computer all day. I'll go to the courthouse myself."

She looked pointedly at the black T-shirt he was wearing. "I hope you're planning to change your shirt before you leave here." Today he was wearing one that advised Remember my name. You'll be screaming it later. Dropping her gaze to her desktop, she began straightening folders. There was no reason, none at all, for her to be embarrassed by the suggestive wording. She thought…she was almost certain…she hadn't uttered his name even once while they were on the couch Saturday night, much less screamed it.

She dug under the sheaf of papers for a list, then handed it to him. "Here's a list of engagements I've wangled invitations to. A little discreet checking proved that one or more of the Garvey descendants is on the guest list. Whether or not you want to accompany me will be up to you. I've marked the ones Amanda is expected to attend, in case you want to focus on those."

He looked at the column of events, dismay written plainly on his face. "Will these things be anything like that engagement party the other night?"

"They'll likely be worse," she answered cheerfully. "But you can't beat the contacts. With very little effort, we can pump any number of people about our targets. You never know what might turn up."

He looked, she thought, decidedly unenthusiastic at the prospect. "Couldn't we just tap their phones?"

"Dream on. If you do decide to come along you'll need some new clothes. Pick up a couple of dark-colored suits, shirts and ties and—" her gaze dropped to his scuffed black boots "—some dress shoes. You can charge it on the company card."

"A tie?"

There was a faintly panicked note in his voice. Relenting, she said, "Just get something appropriate, all right? The dress won't be any more formal than it was Saturday." Truth be told, she couldn't even imagine him in anything dressier than he'd shown up in the other night. And if he managed to look any sexier than he had then, she'd have to carry a stick to keep the women away from him.

And it wouldn't hurt to give herself a good rap with it, either, any time she got another bright idea like asking Lucky to sleep with her.

Feeling heat suffuse her cheeks, she stared blindly down at the papers she had spread out in front of her. "Well, if there's nothing else…" Her voice trailed off.

He remained silent, but didn't leave. She could feel his eyes on her, hot and intense. A long tension-filled moment passed. Then another. The paragraph she was pretending to read might as well have been written in Klingon.

Finally she summoned the courage to raise her gaze. "Did you want to say something?"

"No." The answer was uttered quickly enough, grimly enough, to have her suspecting he wasn't any more eager to discuss what had happened between them, or what *hadn't* happened between them, than she was.

"Okay." She stood, went to the coat closet, and took out a bag. Working automatically, she packed it with a small camera, tape recorder, binoculars, notepads and a miniature computer. Going to her desktop PC she picked up the business cards she'd run off this morning, and carefully separated them, tucking them into a small case in her purse. Crossing to the refrigerator, she took out three bottles of water and an apple, very aware that his gaze never left her.

"Are you waiting for me to offer you lunch or something?" Really, why didn't he just go? She was about to jump out of her skin under that brooding, steamy stare.

"Lunch?" Lucky took a quick glance at his watch, noted the time. *"Non,* I don't think I will bother with lunch today." And he'd take a measure of satisfaction at the thought of leaving Charlotte Wheeler cooling her heels while she got used to the idea of being stood up. He'd never been one to respond to commands.

Reluctantly, he pushed away from the table, headed for the door. Watching her move around the room gracefully, seemingly oblivious to him, wasn't improving his mood any.

She said nothing as he left, and he got as far as his own office, before the frustration bubbled, threatened to erupt. *"Merde."* Turning on his heel, he strode rapidly back to her office, pushing the door open with the heel of his hand and sending it bouncing off the opposite wall. "The hell with this," he growled, stalking toward her.

Looking wary, she rounded the desk, stood clutching the back of her chair. "What's gotten into you?"

"I'll tell you what has gotten into me. You." He slapped the file folder on her desk with enough force to have her wince. "Ignorin' what happened isn't going to work. We have to get this out in the open."

"What's so great about it being out in the open?" she muttered.

"What happened Saturday night," he paused as his excellent memory supplied him with instant mental flashes of the night in question, "shouldn't have happened. It won't again." He thought, he hoped, that if he uttered the words with enough vehemence, they just might be true. "We are friends, you and me. I don't know how that happened, but it did. We aren't goin' to screw that up. For us, sex is off the table. Do you understand?"

He glared at her, daring her to disagree. But she just stood there, with a tiny little smile on her face. He turned to go through the door again, when her voice stopped him.

"I understand perfectly, and I think you do, too. If you're honest, you'll admit it. For us, sex will never be off the table."

He was still standing speechless in the doorway when she brushed by him holding her suit jacket and bag and walked, with a decidedly feminine sway to her hips, out the front door.

Jacey had made several phone calls earlier that day, setting up her pretext for approaching Mark Garvey's neighbors. After another quick call had ascertained that he was at work, she drove out to the upper-class neighborhood where he had a home. Houses in the area sold for upwards of a million dollars, so it would appear that the man was doing very well for himself.

Starting at the house next to his, she knocked on the door and waited until a uniformed maid opened it. "Good afternoon." She presented the woman with a phony business card. "May I speak with the owner, please?"

"Un momento." While the maid went to summon

her employer, Jacey looked casually up and down the street. It wasn't a gated community, which made things a bit easier for her. But there were discreet signs of neighborhood security. She noted one unmarked sedan cruising by, the driver watching her. Most of these areas had a no-soliciting policy, which was why she'd put a Triad Realty magnetic sign on her car door. The security guard would be hard-pressed to decide she didn't have a legitimate reason to be there.

A matronly woman in her midfifties opened the door, looking vaguely impatient. "I'm afraid we aren't in need of a Realtor." She made as if to close the door.

"But isn't this 1018 Vine?" Jacey looked down at her notepad again, pretending to be puzzled.

"Yes, but my house isn't for sale. Nor am I interested in listing it."

"Well, that is odd. This is the address that my partner wrote down. Bruce Cambridge? He said he spoke to someone just last night. Could it have been your husband?"

"Ex-husband, and it sure better not have been." Temper snapped in the lady's brown eyes, and she pulled the door open a little wider. "I got the house and one of the cars in the divorce, and he got the beach home and his triple-D bimbo." She peered suspiciously at the scrawled address on the pad. "I wouldn't put it past him to try something underhanded."

The last thing Jacey wanted was to start some minor war between the stranger and her ex. She gave a wry smile. "Oh, I wouldn't worry. This isn't the first time I've been unable to read my partner's handwriting. See?" She turned the notepad so the woman could look. "I suppose that 8 could be a 6."

"Or a 9," the woman said doubtfully. "My ex had lousy handwriting, too. Caused all kinds of problems over the years, I can tell you."

Because she was afraid the lady would do just that, Jacey attempted to sidetrack her. "Maybe it's the house next door." She indicated Mark Garvey's stately pillared home. "Could that be? Have you heard anything about your neighbor wanting to move?"

"Mr. Garvey?" The woman stepped out on the front porch and looked over at the home, pursing her lips. "I haven't heard a word about it, but he keeps to himself. He used to chat with my ex occasionally. I never did understand why a man alone wanted to keep a house that size. It's not like he's home a lot."

"That's a shame." Jacey eyed the house assessingly. "These homes seem ideal for entertaining."

"He hasn't entertained much since his divorce two years ago. The only people I see over there these days are his family. He's got a brother and a sister, I think, and a younger cousin. He never was on very good terms with his father, from what my ex told me once." She lowered her voice. "That cousin of his is no good, from what I hear. Mark tried to work with him a few years ago, straighten him out, but I don't know how much success he had." She shrugged. "Too much money can ruin people, you know? Lately Mark's had a string of girlfriends who have come and gone, but like I say, he's not around all that much anymore. Maybe he is planning to sell. I can't remember the last time I saw him to speak to."

It was doubtful the woman could give her any other information, so Jacey turned to go. "Well, as long as I'm here I'll drop my card off at a few houses. Thank you for your time."

Aware that the woman was still watching her, Jacey gave a friendly wave and headed off for the Garvey house. Unlike its neighbor, no servant answered the door here. After waiting a few moments she went to the house on the other side, and walked through the same routine, with even less success. The housekeeper told her the owners weren't at home, and since the retired couple had only lived there six months, Jacey doubted they'd be able to provide much useful information.

As she got into her car, she noticed the same dark sedan driving slowly by. It had been no more than fifteen minutes since she'd first seen it. She made a mental note. She might need to remember the security layout before she was through checking out Mark Garvey, so she drove around the neighborhood until she found a house for sale, then jotted down the address and Realtor's phone number.

She waited until she was several blocks away to stop and take the signs off the rental car, and then called the Realtor. By pretending an interest in the house for sale, she was able to glean a great deal of information, with a few nuggets about the neighborhood security that might well come in handy.

Checking her watch, she figured she had a couple of hours before Mark Garvey would be getting off work. Although surveillance was her least favorite part of the job, she thought it would be interesting to see where he spent his free time, and with whom. According to his neighbor, he didn't seem to spend much of it at home. She had descriptions of his cars from her database search. It would be easy enough to tail him from work, although if he headed home, it would be too risky to follow. She couldn't take the chance of being identified by him.

On her way across town, her cell phone rang. She took the precaution of checking the number. Jacey didn't consider it cowardly to be avoiding her mother's calls. It was just a matter of self-preservation.

Seeing her office number listed on the caller ID, she answered, recognized her secretary's voice. "Hi, Joan. What's up?"

"I just thought I should let you know you have a potential client who is in a real rush to get in touch with you."

Pleased, Jacey looked in the rearview mirror, then switched lanes. "That's good news. Is Lucky back yet?"

Traffic was horrific. Slowing to a crawl, she mentally re-estimated the amount of time it would take her to reach Garvey's workplace. What used to be traffic hour years ago had extended to traffic three hours. The summer months were even worse, with the tourists pouring into the area. "You'll have to take a number and I'll return the call when I can."

"That's just it, Jacey." Joan lowered her voice. "She won't be put off. She's called twice and stopped in once. And she says she's coming back and will just wait for your return."

Frowning, Jacey asked, "Did she give a name?"

"She did when she was here. It was—" there was a pause as if Joan was checking something "—Lianna Wharton."

Jacey stilled. J. Walter Garvey's daughter? What in heaven's name would she be wanting? She knew the woman to speak to, of course, but she'd certainly never sought Jacey out before. The fact that she chose to do so now, when Jacey was investigating Lianna's family, was a little too coincidental to be trusted.

"I think I'll swing by the office, speak to her myself," she said. "If she comes back, have her wait."

Disconnecting, she waited impatiently for traffic to allow it, and turned a corner, heading back toward her office. She glanced at the cell phone again, half tempted to call Lucky and run the latest turn of events past him. But after a few moments she thought better of it. She'd never seen him in a blacker mood than he'd been in that day, and she had a strong suspicion that her last remark to him just might have pushed him a little closer to the edge.

Her lips tilted. The role of seductress was new to her, but it wasn't nearly as embarrassing as it could have been. She didn't think she'd ever seen him speechless before. His reaction to her last statement had been memorable.

A couple of miles later, traffic thinned a bit. It would still take half an hour to reach her office, and her mind drifted. Like metal filings to a magnet, it returned to the memory of Saturday night. She recalled the look on his face before he'd pulled away from her. Hunger. A shiver skated over her skin at the memory of the savage expression he'd worn. As if not reaching for her again had been tearing him apart. As if there had been nothing but a rapidly shredding resolve that had kept him from finishing what they'd started, in the most satisfying way possible.

Her throat went abruptly dry. In moments like these, when she actually had time to think about it, she could almost fear the fierceness of the longing she'd seen on his face. But there was also an answering desire within her, an awareness that wasn't going to go away, despite Lucky's unwillingness to address it.

The only question that remained was whether she was going to pursue the issue.

Mingled excitement and trepidation had her stomach hollowing out. She could safely say she would never have mentioned the proposition if she hadn't been… somewhat more relaxed than usual. Okay, tipsy, even. But she wasn't under the influence of any alcohol now, and she wasn't having any luck shaking the idea from her mind. And she laid the blame for that squarely at his feet.

She'd never been particularly susceptible to his brand of charm before, had she? Oh, she'd been aware he possessed it. She was still female, Peter's opinions to the contrary. There wasn't a woman alive who could ignore the wicked promise in Lucky's eyes, the element of danger underlying the charisma. But she'd considered herself somehow immune, as if by identifying it, acknowledging it, she couldn't be touched by it on any level.

He'd played the part of her lover so convincingly Saturday night, his pretense had surely been responsible for putting the thoughts in her head. And even now, aware of all the logic of his arguments against her proposition, the specter of the idea remained, and refused to be banished.

A horn blared, startling her. She had been so engrossed in her thoughts that she hadn't noticed the light turning to green. Proceeding across the intersection, she deliberately forced her mind away from the man weighing on it. She'd do best to concentrate on her upcoming meeting. She had a feeling that it was going to prove very informative.

* * *

Lianna Garvey Wharton was seated in the small waiting area when Jacey pushed open the door. Joan, her usually unflappable secretary, threw her a relieved look. "I had Ms. Wharton wait, as you requested, Ms. Wheeler."

"Lianna." Jacey crossed to the woman with her hand extended. "It's good to see you again. I don't remember the last time we ran in to each other."

Her first thought upon seeing the woman was that life had been unkind to her recently. Her hair was still a carefully coiffed blond, her figure still petite. But she had a brittle air that had been absent the last time they'd met, and her answering smile seemed forced. Her voice was the same, however, high, with a syrupy sweetness that never failed to grate. If she remembered correctly, Lianna had a shrill laugh that could break glass.

Jacey made a mental note to be sure not to amuse her.

"Jacinda, you look wonderful. Just wonderful." Lianna clasped both her hands in her own and surveyed her. "And how clever you are with your business and the new mysterious man in your life." She wagged a finger at her. "I couldn't make it to Peter Brummond's engagement party, but I heard all about your appearance there."

Great. With effort, Jacey ignored her secretary's quizzical look and steered the woman toward her office. "Why don't you come in and tell me all about it?" The last thing she needed was for Joan to get wind of the pretense Lucky had engaged in for her benefit. That would make the working relationship in their office almost impossible.

She seated Lianna at the curved-leg table near her desk and closed the door. "Can I get you some coffee?"

"That would be wonderful. I'm afraid I'm at my wit's end. Caffeine just might calm my nerves."

Keeping her expression carefully blank, Jacey poured a cup and handed it to her. Then, sitting across from her, she said, "So, how can I help you?"

The woman sipped daintily from her cup. "I just can't get over how grown up you've become." She waved a hand when Jacey would have looked away. "Oh, you know mothers. We always think of our children as infants. Why, my Jeffrey can't be more than a few years younger than you, and every time I notice what a fine man he's become it's a new shock." Her gaze was sharp. "You haven't met my Jeffrey, have you?"

Adrenaline began to hum in her veins. She wasn't certain yet just what game they were playing, but she knew they were engaged in one. "I don't believe I have. Does he live around here?"

"He just finished college last year with a degree in international studies." Her voice, her face, were alight with genuine maternal pride. "His father and I had a…difficult marriage, but you'd never know it to meet Jeffrey. He's as well-adjusted as a young man could be. He's working with my father, you know. Learning the business from the ground up, as J. Walter likes to say." There was just a tinge of bitterness in the words. "But family means everything to Jeffrey, so he doesn't mind beginning at the bottom."

"He sounds very…industrious."

"He is. Extremely so. But it wasn't him I came to talk about. It's my father." Her blue eyes suddenly swam with tears. Jacey decided that it must be due to a flaw in her make up that they left her unmoved. "He's dying."

Jacey's shock wasn't feigned, even if it stemmed from a different reason than Lianna might have expected. Had J. Walter decided to tell his family about his illness after all? "I'm sorry to hear that." She didn't have to manufacture the sympathy in her voice. For the first time felt a measure of empathy for the woman before her. Whatever the dynamics of their family, it was never easy to lose a loved one.

"I found out quite by accident, but when I confronted him with the news he refused to give me any details." She pressed her lips together. "We've never been on the best terms, but at a time like this, most people would want their relatives near them, for support, if nothing else. But not J. Walter."

"What can I do, Lianna?"

"I want the details on his health. I'm family, I deserve to know the truth, to prepare for the worst." There was a sparkling teardrop clinging to the edge of the woman's lashes. Then she blinked, and it traced artfully down one smooth cheek.

Jacey got up silently, brought a box of tissues to the table and set them in front of the woman. She wondered distantly if there was some class she'd missed at Miss Denoue's School of Deportment on crying prettily without leaving a ravaged face. How was it that most of her acquaintances had mastered the art, while she couldn't accomplish the feat without smeared makeup and a red nose to show for it?

"I'm just beside myself." The woman was dabbing at her eyes. "I've called the hospital, but I can't get any information from them. They keep reciting some policy or regulation for refusing to talk to me."

"The Health Insurance Portability and Accountability Act would prohibit them from discussing your father's health with you, if he requested them not to do so."

"Yes, that's what they keep telling me. But there must be some way around that. I have rights, too!" Her eyes flashed, and she set her mug on the table with a little more force than necessary. "There are arrangements to be made and I don't even know how much time we're working with. There must be some way around this ridiculous law."

"I believe there are certain exceptions to it, but I'm really not familiar with them. A lawyer could best advise you."

The woman hesitated, and Jacey was given the distinct impression that they still hadn't touched on the real reason for this visit today. But the next statements revealed her purpose all too clearly. "My father…is a difficult man, as well as a private one. I need to know what he's planning for…after he's gone." She gave Jacey a commiserating smile. "Financial details are so tacky, but totally necessary. I'd be willing to make it worth your while if you could uncover any of those details for me."

"You mean you want a copy of his will?"

"Anything that would give me a clue about his intentions. I just need time to ensure that his wishes can be carried out." As if on cue, her eyes filled again. "One of the comforts when losing a loved one is making sure that all is as they would wish it. But with him being so secretive, I can't even help with that."

Jacey wasn't sure whether to roll her eyes or applaud. The woman couldn't be more transparent if she were made of glass. She shook her head. "I'm sorry, but the majority of my job deals with poring over public records." She was deliberately vague. "Wills don't fall into that category. Is there anyone else you think he might have confided his intentions to?"

"I'm not sure." Her blue gaze, teary just a moment ago, had gone steely. "But my father never reveals everything, only enough to get the job done. I know of no one who would be privy to all the facts of the matter."

Her patience at an end, Jacey rose. "Then I'm afraid I can't help you. Perhaps there's a clergyman your father would feel comfortable talking to? If you're worried about him dying without notifying anyone about his wishes, I mean."

From the look on Lianna's face, she recognized that Jacey was being deliberately obtuse, but wasn't sure how to call her on it. "That's an idea. I'll follow up on it. We could be such a comfort to him, Jeffrey and I, if he'd just allow us. J. Walter should be spending this time readying his successor, instead of pushing his family away." She trailed behind Jacey to the door, then paused before leaving the outer office. "But if you reconsider, Jacinda, my offer stands. I'd be willing to pay handsomely for the kind of information that would help me assist my dear father in his final days."

Chapter 8

"So she was fishin'."

"And very frustrated when I didn't take the bait." Jacey leaned back in her chair, surveying Lucky from across her desk. He was slouched in a chair, one ankle hooked comfortably over his knee as he listened to the details about Lianna Wharton's visit. "Something tipped her off, though. It had to have. Finding out about J. Walter's health is one thing. Connecting the dots between him and me is quite another."

"No chance she came to you for the same reason he did. Because she didn't know and trust anyone else in the business."

It wasn't a question, but she shook her head anyway. "Too coincidental, don't you think? I called J. Walter after she left and he said he hadn't told her anything.

Based on my experiences with her, I'd say she wasn't above some snooping."

"If her son works in the business, he might be the one doin' the snoopin' for her." He leaned forward and snatched the apple off her desk, the one she'd put in her bag today and had never gotten a chance to eat.

She sent him an arch look for his high-handed action, but said only, "Garvey's copy of the contract between us is stored in the safe in his office."

Lucky began to toss the apple from one hand to another. "If someone has the combination to his safe, Garvey's got bigger problems than the one you reported."

"He didn't seem to think that was the case. He was more irritated than anything." The word was a masterful understatement. The man had been positively irate. "He thought Lianna might have found out about his condition from listening to his phone messages at his home. The doctor's office had left one about his most recent lab results. He's convinced that the only way someone could have seen a copy of the contract is while it was awaiting his signature on his desk."

"That couldn't exactly put his mind at ease. Like livin' in a pit of vipers."

She thought the man was probably used to it, but it saddened her to think that he had to guard against the same sort of espionage in both business and family. "At any rate, this isn't a disastrous development, but it might be one that complicates things."

He tossed the apple up in a dizzying spiral, caught it with his other hand. "Maybe so, but after what I found out today about Amanda Garvey-Smythe-Collins-Langlois-Pritchard soon-to-be Beauchamp, I'd say Lianna could take lessons on complications from her niece."

Interest spiked. "You got a look at the divorce decrees."

"Lots of reading with four of them. My eyes nearly bled pagin' through them all."

With a quick glance she discounted his claim. He didn't look any the worse for wear despite his afternoon spent at the courthouse. He had taken her advice and changed his shirt, for which she was thankful. Shortly after he'd started work there she'd stocked up on plain black T-shirts to keep at the office. But that hadn't seemed to discourage him from wearing his favorite ones to work. Because she suspected he did it to get a rise out of her, she tried to hide her distaste for them, but was rarely successful.

His mood seemed dramatically improved from the dangerous one he'd sported that morning. She wasn't quite sure what to make of that.

"And?" she prompted.

"Me, I'm an admirer of women with disgracefully low standards." The long slow smile he shot toward her had her temperature notching up a few degrees. "But our Amanda seems to have bad judgment, as well."

"With four exes, that seems a foregone conclusion."

He took a healthy bite out of the apple, chewed and swallowed. "She took a hit on the first marriage. Paid through the nose on alimony. Seems none of the guys she chooses make a lot of money of their own. A few years back she sold the business she had, gave husband number one half to pay him off for good, and then started up the one she heads now."

"The financial report on her firm is solid. She must

be a good businesswoman." She stopped, raised her brows. "You found that in a divorce decree?"

"Oui." He wore a lazy, self-satisfied look. "Full financial disclosure is a wonderful detail, but not the most interestin' one buried in the court proceedings. Apparently she had the bad luck to marry two abusers, an adulterer and a penny-pinchin' cross-dresser. Want me to continue diggin' or do we strike her from the list?"

"I don't think we should discount her yet, although I can only imagine what J. Walter thinks about her marital tag team."

"Any word yet on Stephen Garvey?"

Jacey shook her head. "If my contact in the FTC clears him, he or Mark would be the logical choice to take over for J. Walter."

"Anythin' pop on the NEXIS searches for either of them?"

"I only have a preliminary on Mark done, but I'm going through it now." She indicated the pile of paper she'd downloaded. The database was a compilation of anything that had ever been publicly printed about an individual. Given the prominence of the family name, the material was substantial. The copies would be combed for known associates, affiliations, business connections and social contacts from which they could select sources to follow up on.

Lucky cast an unenthusiastic glance at the sheaf of papers. He'd never made any pretense about his dislike for the more mundane aspects of their job. He was an expert at avoiding them whenever he could. As he'd often told her, he was a man of action.

Heat balled in her stomach. She had first-hand

knowledge that when it came to action, he was quite expert, indeed.

She looked at the clock on the wall. "I'd thought about doing a little surveillance on Mark Garvey, try to get a clue as to where he spends his time after work. According to his neighbor, he's not home much."

"You'll never make it down there by the time business hours are over."

She gave a mental shrug. It could wait. "In that case, I think I'll make an appearance at the New Orleans Civic League gathering tonight. It's just cocktails prior to an awards ceremony, then I'll probably come back here and go through his NEXIS more thoroughly."

Aware of her eyes on him, Lucky made a show of eating his apple, as if that task required a great deal of concentration. When he looked up to catch her eyes on him, he frowned, feeling hunted.

"Any function with the word civic in it is bound to be *rahdoht*." And he'd rather stick a needle in his eye than engage in endless boring conversation with a bunch of strangers who might or might not have anything of interest to impart. "What are you hopin' for?"

"Mark Garvey's ex-wife Tara is the co-hostess. With any luck, I can get a few minutes alone with her. The guest list also includes Stephen Garvey, so I thought it might yield something useful."

Something useful. In terms of the contacts they might make she was right. But he wasn't sure how wise it was to spend any more time than necessary in her company right now. He'd gained a little perspective, spending the afternoon away from her. At least, he thought it was perspective. The bolt of frustration that had been riding him for two long nights had at least subsided a bit. But he didn't think it was particularly wise to put it to the test by watching her all evening, laughing and flirting in a dress showing far more of her charms than he needed to be reminded of right now.

"It's business dress, if that makes you feel any better."

His gaze flew to hers, amazed that she seemed to have plucked the thought from his head. "What?"

Her expression was amused. "You don't have to dress up, if that's what's holding you back. I'm not even changing. I'll bet you didn't order any clothes, did you?"

"As a matter of fact, you're wrong." The surprise on her face brought him a measure of satisfaction. "It was supposed to be delivered this afternoon."

"Maybe it came while I was out. Well, that's settled, then. You're coming."

He hesitated a moment, and then the instant seemed to stretch until the silence was a taut, thrumming alive thing between them. Poring over records all day had given him way too much time to think. He'd been afraid that getting involved intimately with her would take their relationship to a point of no return. It would be, he'd decided, like learning to ride a bicycle backwards. How did they go back to being friends once they'd been, however briefly, lovers? Would a few weeks of wild passionate sex satiate the desperation in his blood, or would it be a constant brutal reminder of what could never be again?

There were few things in this life he feared. But if engaging in an intimate relationship with Jacey, no matter how gut-wrenchingly satisfying it would be, meant he'd lose her completely in the end, he wasn't willing to risk it.

"If you're afraid for your virtue, don't be," he heard her say. Incredulous, his eyes narrowed as she continued, a cool little smile on her lips. "I rarely proposition the same man more than once in the same week. You're safe for several more days, at least."

Was she actually mocking him for his restraint? *Bon Dieu,* but the woman didn't know when to step quietly around a frustrated man.

He bared his teeth in response. "It's not my safety you should be worried about, darlin'. It's yours. Keep pushin' and you might find yourself with more trouble than you can handle."

Shoving himself out of the chair, he stalked out of the office. But not out of the building. *Non,* he wasn't a complete fool, even when he realized how blatantly he was being manipulated. He'd change his clothes and accompany her tonight and while there he'd do the job he was paid for.

And if she was fortunate, if they were both fortunate, the tenuous leash he had on his control just might hold for the duration of the evening.

The ride across town to the hotel where the event was hosted was accomplished in simmering silence. It was, Jacey thought, sneaking a peek at Lucky as they entered the decorated conference room, rather like baiting a tiger. She shouldn't be shocked when he snarled back.

And she shouldn't be tempted to keep pushing until he pounced.

Swallowing, she looked away. Nothing in her experience had prepared her for dealing with a man like him. He cared nothing for the social niceties that glossed the interactions of most of the men of her acquaintance. His emotions, when provoked, would be immediate, unguarded and, more to the point, genuine.

Which made experiencing his passion all the more devastating.

To keep her gaze away, she stared blindly at the crowd already gathered. He wasn't dressed all that differently from the other night, in that he'd chosen black dress pants, and a dark collarless silk-blend pullover. But the jacket this time was the color of wheat, providing an eye-catching contrast to the dark clothes and his dusky complexion. Certainly several heads turned in their direction when they entered.

Spying Tara Garvey talking animatedly to someone across the room, she said in an undertone, "I'm going to mingle. Mark Garvey's ex-wife is the redhead over there in black, and I think that's Stephen Garvey in the corner speaking to the man in the red tie."

"Don't worry about me." His voice was easy, but the gleam in his eye warned her that his temper hadn't yet passed. "I'll be fine on my own."

Taking him at his word, she moved away, with more than a little relief. She wasn't sure just where this new impulse to needle him sprang from, but she was beginning to realize that he was right; it wasn't safe.

Not because she feared him. For some curious reason that she'd never quite understood, she'd long trusted Lucky in a way she had no other. But stirring up this constant tension between them was putting a strain on their relationship, both working and personal. She was going to have to take his advice, and try to back away from the memories that haunted her every time she closed her eyes. Try to forget the press of his body against hers, the hunger of his mouth, the smooth heated skin of his chest.

She took a shaky breath of resolve. If he could set them aside so easily, how difficult could it be?

It took several minutes to make her way across the room and get Tara's attention. When she did, she returned the woman's hug. She'd first met her several years ago when they'd worked on a committee, and always had enjoyed her company. She possessed a droll wit and a sharp mind.

They engaged in chitchat for a few minutes, before Jacey said, "I see on the program that you're up for one of the awards this evening. Congratulations."

Tara smiled and shrugged. "I feel like I should give them the award. Lord knows, I've been glad to be busy the last couple years."

Jacey squeezed her hand. "Are things going better?" Rumor had it that the divorce had been a difficult one.

"Not bad. I'm seeing someone now, so that lifts my self-confidence out of the Dumpster where Mark left it." Tara grimaced. "Not that I can blame him totally for that, but I'm not yet past the bitter stage, I'm afraid. I never actually caught him cheating, but I was pretty sure that was what was going on."

"Oh, I'm sorry, I hadn't heard that."

The woman shrugged and sipped from the glass of mineral water she was holding. "Well, it's not as if the whole family is a model for fidelity. I understand Rupert's new conquest is thirty years his junior. He's invested in some thoroughbred operation of hers, apparently. I'm sure it won't last. They all run through sexual partners like most people do tissues. Well, Stephen's the exception, I guess," she corrected herself. "He's something of a workaholic but a real family man, nonetheless. Believe me, there were many times I envied his wife that."

"What made you think Mark was cheating?" Jacey's stomach knotted at the thought of pumping a woman she respected about her personal life. But it would be hard to find a better source on Mark Garvey than his ex-wife.

"It was little things, you know? Too many late nights to really be working late, callers who hung up when I answered the phone, and large sums of money unexpectedly missing from our accounts." Tara's eyes flashed. "Whoever she was, she must have gotten some hellacious jewelry."

Jacey made a mental note to check more closely on the women Mark had been dating. From what his neighbor had told her, there had been a string of them, so he obviously hadn't stayed with whoever he'd been seeing before the divorce.

"But you're happy now, right?" she asked with genuine concern.

"Getting there." Tara leaned over and gave her another hug. "Thanks for asking. I'm at least content. And back to feeling female enough to have noticed your entrance. Good Lord, girl, what have you gone and gotten for yourself?"

If it had been someone else Jacey would have stiffened in embarrassment, or engaged in the polite verbal jousting that often accompanied such questions. But Tara's tone was playful, and her interest real. And, truth be told, Jacey just plain liked the woman. Always had.

So she turned in the direction of Tara's avid gaze, and looked at Lucky, who appeared to be quite comfortably chatting with Madonna Wilcox, an octogenarian who still managed to attend almost every event Jacey did. The sight of him ignited a slow burn in the pit of her belly that she was helpless to douse.

"He does tend to stand out from the crowd, doesn't he?" she murmured.

"Stand out? Honey, the rest of these men fade to insignificance around him, and I'm including my date. Who is he and where did you find him?"

At that moment Lucky looked up, and catching her gaze on him gave her a steamy stare that told her he still hadn't forgotten their conversation at the office.

"Ohhhh." Tara fanned herself with one hand. "I can feel the heat from here. That man oozes sex appeal. Don't those smoldering looks just turn your knees to putty?"

Jacey attempted a smile and deliberately stiffened the knees in question. She didn't even try to answer. She wasn't used to the effect Lucky Boucher was beginning to have on her. But her knees were the least of her worries. The man was affecting her entire system. And she wasn't quite sure what she was going to do about it.

It was a couple of hours before the congratulatory speeches and spates of polite applause were winding down. Lucky couldn't quite recall what the awards had been for. He hadn't exactly been paying attention. No matter how he tried to focus on something other than the woman at his side, his mind had a way of circling back to her. And that couldn't be tolerated.

There had never been a woman alive who had demanded that kind of hold on his attention. Never been one to burn a brand in his brain—and lower—that had him thinking of nothing but her. A month ago, even a week ago, he would have been amused at the thought. But he was very much afraid that was happening to him now.

He didn't recognize the phenomenon. He damn sure didn't like it. No female tied him in knots. But then, this wasn't any other woman, it was Jacey. There was no walking away from her. No way to rid himself of the frustration riding him by steeping himself deep inside her and letting the torch of desire burn itself out.

Knowing that, accepting it, just made it flame hotter.

He glanced at her profile as she politely listened to the old lady who'd bent his ear earlier for nearly fifteen minutes before Jacey had rescued him. Her face was set in the smooth expressionless mask he was beginning to realize that she donned especially for engagements like this. She'd looked like that much of the first several months they'd worked together, until he had found himself saying things, doing things for the express purpose of forcing some real emotion from her.

And emotion he'd gotten. There was fire there beneath the reserve, and a humor he never would have suspected. Both had captivated him from the first. And when she'd become more than just another woman to him, he'd been able to wall off the attraction he felt for her because he hadn't wanted to jeopardize their fledgling friendship.

The wall was still there, he assured himself uneasily. But it was in pretty dismal condition these days.

His cell phone vibrated in his coat pocket and he withdrew it, checked the number. Recognizing it, he answered quickly.

"Luella, where y'at?" He hadn't spoken to his cousin for several weeks. But her voice had his initial pleasure evaporating.

"Lucky, I need to see you right away. I'm sorry, I know I must be interrupting you. I'm so sorry…"

"La-La, calm down," he soothed, automatically using her childhood nickname. "You're not takin' me away from anythin' important. What do you need?"

"I have to see you." There was a hitch in the woman's voice. "Soon. But if you're busy or something just say, and maybe we can…"

"*Mais non,* when have I ever been too busy for family?" Lucky felt Jacey's quizzical look on him as he spoke. "Where should we meet?"

"I'm at a coffee shop called Cyber-City on Tulane."

He glanced at his watch. "It will take me a half hour to get there."

"I'll be waiting." Rather than the relief he'd expected in her tone, it was still jittery, and he couldn't help but wonder what had his usually cheerful cousin so upset. If it had been a problem with one of their family, she would have said. He hoped she wasn't having problems with her boyfriend again. He was getting a little old to slap around punks who couldn't hold their liquor.

Disconnecting, he met Jacey's gaze. "It was my *cousine.* She's in some sort of trouble. I have to go."

She nodded. "I'll take a cab home. Don't worry about me."

Still he hesitated. "Are you sure? Because I could drop you off first."

"No, go ahead. Help your cousin."

He nodded, worry for Luella niggling at him. "All

right. If this doesn't take long I'll come by the office. Help you go through the NEXIS."

Her eyes widened a little. "You must really be feeling guilty. Go ahead. I hope your cousin is okay."

He rose, his mind already on the upcoming meeting. "So do I."

The time it took him to get across town seemed interminable, but once he walked into the coffee shop-slash-Internet café and saw his cousin, something in his chest lightened. He slid into the booth across from her, noted that she didn't meet his eyes.

"La-La, what is it?" He reached across the table, took both hands in his. "You got man trouble again? How many times I gotta tell you, these bums you find, they're no good?"

His words abruptly stopped when her gaze lifted to his. Misery filled their depths. "Lucky, I'm sorry. You don't know…"

"That will be all, Luella. You may go."

Comprehension slammed through him, and with it came a cold-edged fury. He released his cousin's hands, sat back slowly in the booth. Charlotte Wheeler waited while Luella gave him one last beseeching look, then slid out of the booth and hurried out of the café. He remained silent as Jacey's mother seated herself in the place his cousin had vacated, then stared stonily at her until she spoke.

"Well, what did you expect, Mr. Boucher? That I would continue to allow you to ignore me?" She used a napkin to wipe a crumb off the table, then set her purse on top of it. "It has a certain poetic justice, don't you think? Your cousin is the one who put me in touch with you three years ago. It's only fair that she have a hand in my getting rid of you now."

"Fa'true?" He gave her a mocking smile. "Now how you figure on gettin' rid of me? I'm not of the mind to be goin' anywhere."

"The problem with your mind is that you change it without warning." Her green eyes glittered with emotion. "Three years ago I hired you to do a job and you failed. At least, that's what you would have me believe. Now it has become abundantly clear that you just sensed a better deal for yourself and bided your time before making your move."

She unsnapped her purse and took out a manila envelope. Pushing it across the table toward him, she said, "Here's ten thousand dollars. You don't have to finish the job I hired you for then. All you have to do is walk out of my daughter's life. Now. Without a word to her. If you don't take it, I'll tell her exactly what brought you to her office thirty-six months ago."

"Will you?" He propped his elbows on the table and rested his chin on his fists. "That would be a scene I'd pay to see. I'd like to hear you tell Jacey that you hired a man to sabotage her business. That you wanted her scared, terrified even, by the dangers of her profession, dangers I was to create for her benefit." He dropped his arms, leaned across the table, all the loathing he felt for the woman alive in his face. "Me, I think she needs to know. I'd like to be there when she finds out that her mother would stop at nothin' to destroy her dreams. That you're so selfish you were willin' to sacrifice her happiness for your precious name."

There was a flicker in her eyes that in anyone else might have been mistaken as guilt. He knew the woman well enough to know that was impossible. "Thanks to you, our family name is being held up for ridicule and scorn. I imagine you think that by seducing my daughter you will get your hands on far more money than this. But you need to remember that if I tell her the truth, she'll cut you out of her life, and you'll get nothing." She nudged the envelope closer toward him. "Better to take what you can now, and get out."

He stared at the envelope. He didn't doubt that it was stuffed with a neat pile of bills that would pay the rent on his apartment for years. And he wasn't tempted in the least to pick it up.

His gaze rose to rest on her face. "I've only known Jacey for three years, and I know her better than you ever will. You don't want to understand her, you just want to control her."

"Jacinda," she said with emphasis, "is strong-willed, but she also has enough pride to shut you out of her life if she learns the truth. I'm her only family, she'll eventually forgive my motives. But you…" She pursed her lips, swept him with a disparaging look. "You are dispensable, Mr. Boucher. Are you willing to take the chance that you'll be left with nothing?"

A cold block of ice settled hard and heavy in his chest. "Despite my nickname, I'm not much of a gambler." He waited for the triumphant little smile to cross her lips before he added, "But I know enough about cards to recognize when my opponent is bluffin'."

He waited for her to blanch before he rose. "Do your

worst, Ms. Wheeler. Somehow I think you know that you'll be the big loser in all this if you go through with it."

Striding out of the café, he pushed open the door, hauled a huge breath of air into his strangled lungs. He walked to his car, unlocked it, then yanked open the door, slid behind the wheel. Currents of rage were speeding along his nerve endings, fiery circuits of fury that had him longing to smash something. Anything. Years ago he'd have headed to the nearest tavern, taken his temper out on the first person who looked at him wrong.

But a lot had changed in the last few years. He wasn't the same man he'd been back then. He wasn't always sure just who he was now, but he was far different from the man who had walked into Jacinda Wheeler's office with the intention of sending her running home to her *maman* within the month.

And if he'd changed, Jacey had had a lot to do with it.

He turned the key in the ignition, shifted the car into gear. Charlotte must be desperate to make a threat like this, especially when he was fairly certain she had no intention of going through with it. She couldn't expose his original intentions without exposing her own, and she wasn't about to take that kind of risk.

Broodingly, he checked the rearview mirror and switched lanes, heading for the freeway. But for all his conviction, the encounter left a block of foreboding in his chest. He didn't need the woman's reminder about Jacey's reaction if she found out what had really brought him to her office three years ago. She'd slice him from her life in one precise swipe.

And the hell of it was, he wouldn't even blame her.

Chapter 9

Lucky spent most of the next day out of the office, and he was honest enough to admit that it was to avoid the woman he worked for. After lying awake most of the night with the conversation between him and Charlotte Wheeler replaying over and over in his head, he didn't trust himself to face Jacey right away. He needed time and distance to tuck away the twin spears of guilt and remorse. He'd spent most of the night trying to convince himself that it wasn't his initial intentions toward Jacey that counted; it was the relationship that had been forged between them in spite of it.

In the darkest hours before the dawn, he'd almost believed it.

He checked in with Joan, then spent the morning making calls on his cell to former clients of Amanda Garvey's while pretending to be a Human Resources

employee for a hospital in Baton Rouge. The calls didn't
elicit anything but glowing reports of Amanda's firm.
Despite his finessing, none of the contacts were able to
provide any information the least bit personal. He
wasn't discouraged. There were plenty of other sources
that could be tapped to provide them.

When he'd finished, he drove to the building that
housed the woman's offices. In the midst of the business
district, it was on the third and middle floor of a newer
glass-and-chrome building. With some difficulty, he
found a parking spot. He took his digital camera and
hooked a wide strap around it that he slipped over his
head. Then he grabbed a Saints hat, put it on backwards,
and took a quick look in the mirror.

With the grim expression and the unmistakable
marks of a sleepless night, he wasn't sure he'd pass for
a tourist, but he'd learned to play whatever role was
called for at the moment. He walked to the building in
question, and then past it, down the street for several
blocks and back. Only after familiarizing himself with
the area did he pull open the door and walk inside.

He wouldn't have much time before he was approached. High-class places like this didn't allow casual street traffic. He spotted the desk situated several
yards away, with the elevators beyond it. The person
manning the desk would be politely referred to as a security guard, but they were usually glorified reception-
ists, buzzing visitors by once they'd proved a legitimate
purpose for being in the building.

Ignoring the man behind the desk who'd looked up
at his entrance, he slowed, pretended to be examining
the list of building occupants. He was unsurprised to see

the name of Amanda's firm, but the sight of another familiar one had him taking a second look.

"May I help you?"

He turned to greet the guard who was approaching him, and then, as if his feet had gotten tangled in the act, tripped, and nearly fell to the ground. He made a production of saving the camera before he hit the floor, depressing the button to take a shot as it was aimed in the direction of the occupant board. Then, to make it look realistic, he fell to his knees, letting loose a string of mild curses as he did so.

"All you all right, sir?"

It was the man's tone that caught Lucky's attention first. He picked himself up and dusted himself off, appraising the stranger. Far from the slightly bored, yet polite tone he'd expected, this man's voice was tinged with suspicion.

"I'm fine. Think I'm lost, though. I was looking for the Renault Agency. Could you tell me if they're located anywhere around here? I lost the slip of paper that I had the address written on, but I know I've got the street right."

The guard's tone never changed. "I wouldn't know. You won't find that business in this building, however."

"You must have heard of them. They're sports agents. They handle some big-time names, too. As long as I'm in town, I thought I might stop by there, see if I can catch sight of any famous clients comin' or goin'." He patted the camera the way he would a baby. "Folks back home would have to believe me if I showed a picture, right? Sure you don't have any idea where that place might be?"

"No, sir, I'm afraid not."

Lucky grinned at him. The man's expression never cracked. "Guess I'll keep looking then. Sorry to bother you."

He turned and ambled back outside, fully aware that the guard stood staring after him. Heading in the direction of his car, he mused on the surprises the short scene had revealed.

He hadn't expected to find that Stephen Garvey's investment company was located in the same building as his sister's business. Jacey hadn't mentioned it, and he'd been concentrating his investigative efforts so far on Jeffrey and Amanda. But what was even more curious was that the man working the downstairs desk was almost certainly a cop.

Getting in his car, he headed to the office. He was experienced enough at recognizing the type. It had been in the man's eyes, in his manner. There was also the fact that he hadn't had a clue that the Renault Agency was only three blocks down, on the other side of the street. So whatever his purpose there, Lucky doubted he'd been on the job long.

He hadn't had a chance to do more than glance at the rest of the occupant names. When he reached the office he'd download the digital picture onto the computer. He was beginning to wonder if there was any business connection between Amanda and her stockbroker brother. It wouldn't hurt to dig a bit deeper into her finances.

Jacey's car wasn't in the parking lot. Given the time, he guessed that she'd gone to Garvey Enterprises to be in position to tail Mark Garvey after work. She was fairly accomplished at the task, but if the time came that they needed in-depth covert surveillance on any of the subjects, they'd have to contract out for extra help. Either of them ran the risk of being identified.

He downloaded the picture and jotted down each of the building occupant names to be checked later. Then he immersed himself in Amanda Garvey's finances, and by the time Joan's voice finally interrupted him hours later, his shoulders were stiff from poring over the documents. Looking up, he regarded the secretary, who was slinging her purse over her shoulder. "Are you going to work all night? Because I'm heading out. You'll have to lock up."

"I'll take care of it," he promised. "Unless...do you expect Jacey back?"

She shook her head, already turning. "I know she had dinner reservations, so she probably won't be in again tonight."

"Dinner reservations?" Every instinct went on alert. Simple interest, he told himself, as he pushed away from his desk and trailed the woman into the outer office. Certainly not jealousy. He'd never been jealous of a female in his life. "With who?"

"A new client. At least that's the way it sounded from what I heard of the conversation. He seemed quite insistent that they meet tonight."

"What was his name?"

Joan sent him an exasperated look. "What's with the third degree? I'm sure Jacey will tell you all about it tomorrow."

"I'm interested, okay?" He followed her to her desk, where she looked at the appointment book. Running her index finger over the page, she stopped at a name. "Here it is. Vinny Tomsino, is his name."

There was a roaring in his ears, and sheets of ice moved over his skin. "Tomsino?"

"That's right. They're discussing business over dinner, she said. I'm late. Promise to lock up, or Jacey will have my hide."

He nodded distractedly and she left with a wave. He went to the desk and peered down at the appointment book, as if to make sure. But there it was, in Joan's neat handwriting. Vinny Tomsino.

Bracing himself with both hands on the desk, he drew in a deep breath. The man might not be a made wise guy, but he was definitely connected. There wasn't an enterprise he was engaged in that was legit, and Lucky knew that first-hand. There was also little the man wouldn't do to get what he wanted.

If he'd tried, he couldn't have imagined anyone he'd want to keep further away from Jacey.

"What sort of services are you interested in, Mr. Tomsino?"

Jacey sipped from the wine the man had ordered and nodded her approval to the waiter who stood nearby. Like a wraith, he disappeared.

The smile on Tomsino's wide seamed face didn't touch his eyes. They remained watchful. Assessing. Not for the first time since she'd joined him, she had a feeling that she was being weighed and measured. But if he had formed an opinion of her, there was no sign of it in his expression.

She hadn't known what to expect from the brief conversation they'd had on the phone. From the persistent way he'd pressed for this meeting, she'd been left with an impression of a man who was well used to getting his own way. After several minutes in his company, she was no more enlightened.

She hadn't recognized his name when he'd called earlier, and seeing him now, she was certain their paths had never crossed. He wasn't exactly forgettable.

He was no more than six foot, but he had to tip the scales at over three hundred pounds. Even with his girth, however, he gave the impression of strength. And unmistakable aura of power. The wait staff at the restaurant spoke to him with a deference that indicated they knew him well and accorded him a certain amount of respect.

He wore money in the manner of some people who hadn't been born to it. His navy suit was obviously custom-made, and the diamond on his finger bordered on ostentatious. His dark hair was thinning, but immaculately trimmed. But it was rarely the outward trappings that told the most about a person, she'd learned. It was the eyes.

And his dark fathomless gaze revealed nothing. It was as empty, as flat as a shark's. "I'm actually thinking we can help each other." He pushed the menu toward her. "If you like steak, the New York strip here is the best in town."

Flipping open the menu, she glanced over the entrées. There were no prices listed, which always meant those who needed to inquire about them couldn't afford the meal. "Mine is a small firm, but I have several other sources I contract with. So if you're looking for a specialized service, I'm certain we can oblige you."

"That's good to hear. What I'm looking for is real

specialized. And I don't think you'll need to contract out for anything. You've got everything I need."

She gave him a polite smile. "That's good to know. What can I do for you?"

"I'd like you to forward to me all your future reports before sending them to J. Walter Garvey. Then I'll let you know how I want them rewritten."

He raised a finger and as if on cue, the waiter reappeared. Tomsino placed his order calmly, as if his words hadn't struck Jacey completely dumb.

Her mind seemed to have gone numb. Thoughts tumbled incoherently, no single one making logical sense. Icy fingers of shock inched up her spine.

"What about you, Miss Wheeler?" Tomsino's tone was solicitous, as if he hadn't just dropped a bombshell. "Are you going to try the New York strip, too?"

"I'll have the crab legs," she heard herself say evenly. "Caesar salad with the plum dressing. No potato."

She waited for the man to scribble down the order and move away, before forcing herself to meet Tomsino's gaze again. "I'm afraid I don't know what you're talking about."

"You do." His voice was almost gentle, his gaze anything but. "The old man's going to die, and he's looking for someone to take over for him. I've got someone in mind and I'll save you a lot of time and effort by telling you who you'll recommend. All that you'll have to do is fake some more reports, sit back, collect the old man's money and what I'm going to pay you, as well."

"Why would you think I'm working for Mr. Garvey?" There was a flare of anger, melting some of the frost that had encased her system.

"I don't *think*—I know. We can spend the rest of the meal dancing around it, but we both recognize that I'm right. Just like we both know you're going to do exactly as I say."

She reached for her glass, brought it to her lips and sipped again, distantly pleased that her hand wasn't trembling. When she'd replaced the glass on the table, she said, "You seem to be way ahead of me on this one. What gives you the impression that I'm so easily manipulated?"

He picked up the table knife idly, his ring catching the reflection and bouncing off it. "I guess you could say I've been spoiled. Everyone does what I want, Miss Wheeler. Because if they don't, things start going very very bad for them in a hurry."

The waiter came back with a basket of rolls, which he set on the table between them. Tomsino reached for one, broke it in half and began buttering it.

"The problem with being spoiled, Mr. Tomsino, is that you're unprepared for being told no. But that's what I'm telling you." She leaned forward, looked him straight in the eye and said clearly, "No. I don't respond well to threats, and I don't need your money. So whatever scheme you're planning, you'll plan it without me."

Remarkably, he grinned, this time with real amusement. "I like a woman with some backbone," he said, in a tone that had her flesh crawling. "Maybe we can do more business after this deal is taken care of. You'll find that I can be real generous when I get my way."

Revulsion snaked through her. "I'll have to take your word for it, because as far as I'm concerned, our association ends right now."

His cell phone rang in the midst of her words, distracting him. Frustrated, she sat back in her seat as he answered it. He hadn't seemed to be paying much attention to the gist of her message, in any case. She was getting the distinct impression that he was used to steamrollering over any protests.

His phone conversation didn't appear to be making him happy, however. His face was growing red, his responses terse and angry. A sliver of satisfaction lanced through her. It was good to see him thwarted by someone else. He needed to get used to it. Because there was no way she was going to comply with his demands.

When he ended the call she opened her mouth, intent on telling him exactly that. But he was already rising, slipping the cell phone into his pocket. "Something's come up that requires my attention. Feel free to stay and enjoy the meal you ordered."

"That won't be necessary," she said coolly, pushing her seat back. "Our business here was finished anyway."

He leaned over her, one arm braced on the table to prevent her exit. His face shoved close to hers, he said, "It's not healthy to say no to a man like me, Miss Wheeler. I suggest you go home and do some of that investigating you're supposed to be so good at and figure out exactly who you're dealing with here. Maybe when we meet again, your attitude will be different. I hope, for your sake, that it is."

With that he straightened, turned and walked out of the restaurant.

It wasn't until the third try that Jacey was able to fit her key into the lock of her front door. She'd left the restaurant with temper still simmering forty minutes earlier, but on the drive home, she'd noticed with a little shock that her hands had had a tendency to shake as she gripped the steering wheel. The sign of weakness irritated her. Even that small reaction seemed like a victory for the man who'd tried to muscle her, and it was infuriating to give him even that much power.

She set her purse on the gateleg table in the foyer and shut the door behind her. The inviting air of her home failed to calm her as it usually did. She was too busy trying to make sense of the scene that had occurred earlier.

What stake did Tomsino have in the naming of Garvey's heir? And how in heaven's name had the man learned of the case she was working on? Her head ached with the questions that were ricocheting through her mind, none with answers readily apparent.

A hammering on her door jolted her, the sound shattering her thoughts. Her head jerked toward the sound, but she didn't move toward it. What if it was Tomsino? Unease pooled in her belly. She didn't want to face the man again until she was armed with a little more information. Of who he was, first of all. And why he was intent on meddling in the investigation. She was determined to be much better prepared the next time they met. He wasn't a man who should ever be allowed the upper hand.

The pounding started again. "Jacey, open the door. Now."

Relief filtered through her at the familiar voice. She crossed to the door and opened it, standing aside to allow Lucky entry. She didn't even want to admit how happy she was to see him. "You are not going to believe my night."

"You don't think?" He wheeled around then, fixed her with a look. "How 'bout I try? You had dinner with a lyin', thievin', murderin' bastard who's been known to have people killed for standin' in his way." When her jaw dropped, he gave her a hard look. "How'd I do?"

"You know Vinny Tomsino?"

"*Oui.* I do." He balled his fists and shoved them in the pockets of his black leather jacket as if he didn't trust himself not to start swinging. "So I know that you're too far out of your league to realize the danger you're in. I know that if I hadn't gotten him out of there, even now you'd be agreein' to whatever he was demandin', or payin' the consequences."

The rest of his words were lost on her while she keyed in to just a few. "Wait a minute. You got him out of there? How?" Comprehension slammed into her. "That was you on the phone?"

Frustration seemed to shimmer off him in waves. "Let's just say, I got the ball rollin'. And you're missin' the point, darlin'. What the hell were you thinkin', gettin' anywhere near that guy?"

It was obvious to her that Lucky knew a great deal more about the man she'd met with this evening than she did, and the knowledge was annoying. Especially as she realized now that she would have been far better equipped to handle the man had she possessed any of those facts herself.

She started to walk by him. "I thought I was meeting with a potential client. But it wasn't until he started making threats that I realized my mistake."

"Threats?" He grabbed her elbow as she walked by,

whirled her around to face him. "What kind of threats? What did he want with you?"

She searched his face warily. Suppressed fury had tightened his jaw, and his eyes burned with a dangerous light. She rarely had cause to see this side of him, but she knew enough to be wary. "I didn't know who he was. Well, technically I still don't. And he's connected somehow to one of the Garvey heirs." In terse sentences she relayed the gist of their conversation, concluding, "As we suspected, someone has gotten wind of our investigation. And that person is somehow connected to Tomsino. We just have to figure out which one of them it is."

"You're not goin' to have anythin' more to do with this case." His face, his tone, were grim. "I'll take over from here on."

She tried to yank away from him, irritation spiking when she was unable to. "I've had just about enough of being told what to do tonight. I'll see this case through, and I won't be bowing to the likes of Vinny Tomsino, either."

"*Cher,* you don't even know what you're gettin' into with Tomsino, but I do. I'll think of a way out of this, one that will keep you safe. But you'll need to step aside. Let Tomsino deal with me."

"No." Furious, she placed her hands on his chest and gave him a push. "I'm not going to be scared off by some petty crook who thinks he's got a ticket to make a buck off one of my cases."

His dark eyes glittered down at her, his face stamped with frustrated fury. "You don't know what that man's capable of."

"And you do?"

"Oui." The single-word answer was enough to silence her. "I know exactly. I used to work for him."

That shut her up as nothing else could. The thought of Lucky connected in any way to a pig like Tomsino was like a cold splash of water in the face. "Doing what?"

"Bodyguard for some of his girls, mostly. Driver. Odd jobs." He gave a careless shrug that wasn't really careless at all. "Until it became very clear to me that most people who spent any amount of time at all around Tomsino ended up in prison or dead. I didn't care for either prospect. And I'm not about to let you get in over your head on this. You back away from the case and I'll think of a way to get him off your back."

Her head was swimming. The shocks were coming fast and hard, quick sneaky jabs that left her reeling. She'd known Lucky had experience on the rough side of the streets. It was there in his eyes, in the layer of menace that could radiate from him in times of temper. In times like these.

But she wasn't about to quail before his displeasure any more than she had Tomsino's. "I don't like being pushed, Lucky. Tomsino might not know that, but you should. We can think of a way out of this together, one that will expose whichever Garvey has put him up to this, and still protect J. Walter. I owe my client that."

He recognized the stubbornness on her face. He'd seen it enough over the years. A wave of helplessness hit him then, strong enough to stagger him. It was like watching two locomotives hurtling toward each other and being unable to do anything to stop the inevitable collision.

And she…she didn't have the sense to know when to leave well enough alone. Whatever instincts she had should be screaming at her to tread warily. A man in the grip of powerful warring emotions shouldn't be pushed.

But she didn't seem to sense the danger. If she'd had one ounce of self-preservation, she would have read the expression on Lucky's face and backed away, given him a chance to rein them in.

Furious with her, with the entire situation, he answered in the only way he could. By hauling her body up hard against him and pressing his mouth to hers.

Temper was whipping through him, fueled by fear for her. That kind of pent-up emotion demanded a release. Passion dictated the only avenue it could take.

Her flavor raced through his system, inciting an all-too-familiar fire to flame hotter. Wrapping his arm around her waist, he brought her closer. One hand threaded through her hair and he steeped himself in the taste of her.

There was a moment when she was completely still. Frozen by shock, he thought, or fury. He wasn't certain which. Then he felt her hand fist on the front of his shirt, yank him nearer. She made a sound, deep in her throat that caused his pulse to riot.

Her mouth nipped at his, her tongue battling his boldly. She wasn't a passive recipient in any area of her life. He'd damned that quality of hers a moment ago. Now he exulted in it.

He felt her hands shoving his jacket off his shoulders, but he refused to release her long enough to take it off. Her neck was a long sleek line that begged to be explored and his mouth sped down it, then up again. She began to unbutton his shirt, gave up and pulled his shirt from his waistband, skated her hands along his sides.

She tore her mouth free long enough to gasp, "Take your clothes off."

"You first." When she didn't move to obey within the next few seconds his impatience peaked and he stepped back, shrugged out of his coat and shirt and then undid the front buttons on her dress with a speed that drew a laugh from her. The low throaty sound had all his senses roaring.

Her breasts were encased in lace-edged bits of silk. The creamy mounds swelling above the cups would tempt a saint, reward a sinner. The dress framed her slender torso, and the sight of all that bare skin shrouded in fabric was both temptation and torment. He didn't recognize this dark violent need clawing through him. He wanted her bare, under him, surrounding him, now, right now. The urgency was a fist in his gut, clenching more tightly at her answering savage response.

He bent his head to tongue the edge of her breasts where they rose above the scrap of lingerie. She kicked off her shoes, sending them both stumbling. He steadied himself by grasping her bottom, hissed in a breath when her busy hands stroked over his torso, then lower.

His belly quivered. She struggled with his belt, desperation evident in the movements, in the scrape of her teeth along his throat. Her need was arousing, would have been more so if his own wasn't slashing through him like a ruthless blade. He pushed the sleeves of her dress over her arms, reaching behind her to release her bra. Dispensing with that, as well, he busied his hands and mouth with hot, warm flesh.

She was rose-petal soft, silky and fragrant. He rolled her nipples between his thumbs and forefingers before taking one in his mouth, sucking strongly at her. Her back arched, and he feasted on her, driving them both mad with lips and tongue and teeth. He'd dreamed of having her like this, just like this. Mindless and frantic and hungry for him. In his fantasies he'd always harbored more control, showed more finesse. Which meant this couldn't be a fantasy. Because restraint had never seemed further away.

He moved her backwards, only dimly aware of his surroundings, unwilling to stop and get his bearings. They stopped only when a wall was against Jacey's back, and he dropped to his knees before her, using his mouth to explore every curve, each hollow, every inch of smooth scented skin.

Jacey's system was awash in a wild and reckless lust that wouldn't be denied. She kneaded the tight muscles in his shoulders, gasped when he nipped the curve of her waist in response. Impatiently, she tugged at him, urging him higher. She wanted to feel all of him, sleek heated skin pressed against hers, with no clothes between them. She wanted to feel hard male hands streaking over her, a hungry mouth twisting against his own.

She didn't recognize this edgy greed, this wild galloping ride toward madness. Her hands threaded through his hair as he pressed scalding kisses across her stomach. His fingers, those wicked clever fingers, toyed with the lacy tops of her nylons where they ended high on her thighs. Every pulse in her body was throbbing like a wound. Her senses were careening madly, crashing and colliding as sensation slammed into sensation.

It had to be soon. Feeling was leaving her limbs, pooling in the sensitized areas he was devouring with his mouth. He rose and she sighed a grateful breath, reaching to release his zipper with more desperation than finesse. And then she went boneless when he cupped her, his fingers slipping under silk to plunge deep inside her.

His mouth sealed hers, battering her senses in a dual assault and she twisted against him in frenzied need. She was sizzling from the inside out, rocking harder and harder to meet those clever stroking fingers, until she was flung mercilessly over the edge, shock waves of release pulsating through her.

Lucky felt his vision haze as the first climax took her. He'd hungered for her for so long that the desire had become embedded inside him, as natural as breathing. Hearing her broken cries, feeling the slight sting as her fingers clutched his back battered his defenses. His own need was pumping through him, a brutal scream for satisfaction, one he was only going to find buried deep inside her.

He hooked his fingers in the sides of her panties and dragged them over her hips. Jacey arched toward him, her breasts flattening against his chest. She reached inside his open trousers and closed her fingers around him. The air abruptly leached out of his lungs.

Thought all but shattered. He withstood her rhythmic stroking for long moments until the fabric of his control shredded. Operating more on habit than reason, he managed to retrieve a condom from his pocket and put it on, while she shoved his pants down his legs. He grazed the cord of her neck with his teeth, a feral tide of greed rising swift and high.

Her hands raced over his back, and he lifted her, pressing her against the wall. Stepping between her open thighs, he entered her with a long fluid stroke that had their groans mingling.

He barely heard her cries. There was a fierce insatiable need to get deeper, harder, faster. Her legs climbed his, wrapping around his hips, and he thrust, with all the force and primal desire hammering through him. The world had receded. There was only him and this woman, the softness of her body, her tight wet sheath clenching around him.

Her nails raked across his skin and a feral snarl sounded in his throat. He pounded himself into her, wanting, needing to see her eyes as they mated. But the savage greed that had arisen in him blinded him to everything else. All he could do was bury his face in her throat and plunge ever deeper inside her until passion erupted, the climax rocketing through him as he tumbled headlong into pleasure.

Chapter 10

She thought she'd seen stars. She was certain she'd touched them. Jacey was grateful for the unyielding wall at her back, the hard sleek body pressed against hers, keeping her from doing a slow boneless melt into a puddle of satiated hormones. If she'd been able to move she would have stretched like a lazy well-satisfied feline. As it was, she barely had enough energy to slide a hand languidly down Lucky's damp spine, while she waited for strength to return to her limbs.

That had definitely not been sex. She'd had sex before. Performed correctly, the act was enjoyable, mildly arousing, with a pleasant afterglow. This…this had been shattering. A riot of sensation that had assaulted her system. It was the difference, she thought dimly, as Lucky began nuzzling her neck, of setting off Roman candles one at a time, or lighting up the whole boatload of fireworks for one awe-inspiring display. She'd always thought patience was its own reward.

But there was definitely something to be said for avid greed.

His voice was muffled against her skin. "Are we still standin'?"

She smiled, rolled her head to allow him better access. "Kind of."

"Just checkin'. Can't feel my legs."

Slipping her hands down over his firm butt to his hard thighs, she squeezed. "They feel fine."

The nip he gave her then stung, but not enough to motivate her to move. "What are the chances you're going to carry my weak, wrecked body to your *chambre à coucher?*"

She assumed he was referring to her bedroom. Not knowing for sure didn't affect her answer in the least. "Not looking good at the moment."

Heaving a sigh against her, he straightened. "You're a mean woman, *cher.* I don't know when I started findin' that so damn arousin'." Bracing a hand against the wall for strength, he withdrew from her, dispensed with the spent protection and then leaned heavily against her again. "Do we have to climb stairs?"

A laugh bubbled out of her at the note of resignation in his tone. "Maybe we should have thought of that a little earlier."

"Darlin', if you were able to think, we weren't doin' it right." He surprised her then by scooping her up in his arms and striding for the curved staircase. "Maybe we need to try it again. Might need some practice."

The sexy banter, accompanied by the wicked glint in

his eye, made it hard to be self-conscious about the fact
that they were both naked, save for the thigh-high nylons she still wore. "I have a feeling you've had plenty
of practice already."

"Not with you." At the top of the stairs he paused.
"Which way?"

She gestured toward her bedroom door and he turned
to use his shoulder to push it open. A sliver of worry
edged through her feeling of well-being. "What about
what you said before? About our friendship?"

He dropped her on the bed, and dove on top of her,
bracing himself with his hands on either side of her
face. "I don't want to be friends anymore." Ducking his
head, he caught her bottom lip in his teeth, his mouth
muffling her laugh.

If the first time had been frenzied, a headlong rush
into pleasure, this was more leisurely, a thorough explo-
ration of taste and touch and sight. He had the most
wonderful hands, Jacey thought, arching beneath him.
Soothing and tormenting by turn, abrading one moment, smooth the next. He drew the nylons down her
legs, one fraction at a time, his lips exploring each newly
bared inch.

The moonlight slanted through the sheers at the
French doors, washing the bed with splintered shadows.
The lace-edged sheets and piled pillows had always
made the place seem feminine, and now they provided
stark contrast to Lucky's rakish masculinity. He knew
just where to touch her to have her gasping, just how
much pressure to use when he took her nipple in his
mouth and tortured it exquisitely.

They rolled on the bed, into and out of the slivers of

light, bodies sealed together. Breast to breast, hip to hip, legs tangled. Lucky raised himself on one elbow above her to drink in the sight she made bathed in moonlight. Her gold hair spilled against the sheets, silk on satin. With her fair skin she was a study of cream and gold, and he felt something stir in his chest at the picture she made. She was all long lean limbs, luscious curves and exotic scents. And he wanted her, all of her, in a way that went deeper than lust.

He kissed a path down her torso, lingered to explore the crease of her breast, the shallow indentation of her navel. He felt the leap of her pulse beneath his lips, and determined to restrain his own need this time until he could drink in every emotion that took her, savor every response.

But the lady had other ideas. She shifted beneath him and he allowed her to move him to his back, to sprawl on top of him. Then it was his turn to be langorously explored, as she slid clever hands over him, around him. Her mouth trailed over his chest, pausing to scrape one masculine nipple with her teeth, eliciting a quick shudder from him. His response made a mockery of his earlier vow. There was torment there in the sweet soft skin pressing and sliding over his. In the playful fingers that could tease one moment, then return for a firmer caress the next.

Her hair lay like a curtain of silk across his belly, as she dropped moist warm kisses across his heated flesh. He slid his hand from the indentation of her waist, over her hip, reveling in the slender curve of feminity. Then she slipped lower, and his body tensed a moment before she took him in her mouth.

The hot wet suction shot him straight to madness. One of his hands tangled in her hair, the other gripped one round globe of her bottom. He could feel the oxygen searing in his lungs as he fought for air, air that seemed steeped in her scent. Every breath he took he breathed her. Every beat of his heart sounded her name. Her tongue swirled along his length and with each wicked stroke she pushed him just a bit closer to the edge.

Hunger, only recently sated, leaped forth like a wildfire in his blood. Her ravenous mouth drove him to dangerous heights, heights he was unwilling to scale without her with him every step of the way. With a tug on her shoulders he urged her upward and he crushed her mouth with his. A moment later she was tearing away from him, rolling toward the nightstand, fumbling in the drawer for protection.

Her motions were swift and sure as she rolled the latex sheath over him, and his vision hazed as her fingers stayed to stroke, squeezing gently. Then she straddled him, taking his aching length inside her with one fluid move.

She shimmered over him, around him, the delicate pulsations of her inner muscles drawing him deeper. She held a moment, then another, as their bodies both trembled. In the dim moonlight her skin shone like alabaster. The air shimmered with promise.

Then she moved, slowly at first, spinning out the pleasure with each languorous stroke of her body over his. He skimmed his hands over her, the rounded shoulders, the long slender arms, the perfect breasts and narrow waist. Her neck arched, and a sigh shivered out of her.

Quicker now. Harder. Deeper. The pace she set fired

an answering response in his system. He gripped her hips, countered each move she made with an upward lunge that drove him to her center. Every feeling, every sensation, was arrowed where they were joined, friction and heat. She arched her back, riding him, her movements growing wilder with each moment. He dragged his eyelids open, tried to focus. Every motion took her into a sliver of light, back into shadows, the contrast dizzying. Erotic. She set a punishing pace, which he met with every thrust of his hips as the merciless desire battered them.

He watched as the first peak hit her, the flush on her face, the shudders racking her body before his vision blurred. Unwilling to be left behind, he moved up inside her more fiercely, insistently until she crested again, flinging herself forward against him limply. Then with her hair curtaining his face, his hands gripping her hips, his own climax ripped through him. And as he leaped over that final precipice, her name was screaming through his mind.

Lucky drew the sheet more closely around her, then kept his arm around her waist to anchor her next to him. She lay spent and sleeping against him, and it was a curious pleasure to watch her.

In the first weeks after he'd met her, he'd entertained more than a few X-rated thoughts involving her naked and writhing. Then when he'd discovered more with her than he'd found with any other woman, he'd successfully, over time, tucked those mental images away.

Odd then, that the simple act of holding her, hearing the slight sound of her breathing, could be so satisfying.

He lay there, drowsy and contented, while the first layer of slumber hovered over him. Some tiny noise punctured that state, brought him wide awake again in a flash. Listening, he mentally cursed, then disengaged himself carefully from the woman by his side.

Padding downstairs, he searched in the dark for their clothes, managing to find his pants and drag them on. Then he stumbled to the door, flipped on the outside switch and used the peephole to see who would be calling on Jacey after midnight.

He opened the door to Vinny Tomsino, braced one hand against the jamb to bar his entrance. "Funny time for a visit."

If he'd been in the mood he might have been amused by the shock that crossed the other man's wide face, followed by a suspicious expression that was much more familiar.

"Boucher. I didn't even know you were around these parts anymore."

"What I'm wonderin' is, what brings *you* around *these* parts."

The other man craned his neck to look beyond him into the home. Then he looked back at Lucky and smirked, his gaze flicking over him. "Guess some things haven't changed. You always did have a way with women. Even some of my most jaded girls ask about you from time to time." He paused a beat, his eyes glinting in the darkness. "I always tell them you're dead."

"Wishful thinkin' on your part, I expect."

Lucky didn't note many changes in the man. Maybe the wall of muscle had given just a bit more to fat, but he wouldn't ever make the mistake of underestimating him. He could move like a snake when he chose, was just as quick and lethal. And his eyes wouldn't change while he struck. They stayed expressionless whether he was eating a gourmet meal or beating a man to a battered, unrecognizable pulp. Lucky thought he probably still derived the same pleasure from both acts.

"I've got no beef with you, Boucher. Just go and get the lady and disappear while she and I have a discussion."

Lucky swung his head slowly side to side. "*Non*. To get to her you have to go through me. I'm wonderin' if you're ready to do that."

Vinny looked over his shoulder to where the long black stretch limo was idling at the curb. Lucky knew the driver would be armed. He always had been when he'd served in that capacity. He'd heard that the man had begun to travel with a couple of bodyguards, as well. Tomsino had no shortage of enemies.

"Listen." Vinny turned back to face him. "This doesn't concern you, but I'll make it worth your while if you just find yourself another broad for the time being. I wouldn't think this one was much your type, anyway."

Something went cold and hard inside him while he watched Tomsino reach into his suit jacket to withdraw his wallet. It was the second time in as many days that someone had offered to buy him off, and the similarity burned.

"She's not your type, either. This one's got connections at the highest levels in the city, and even you can't touch her without bringin' all kinds of trouble down on yourself. Can your organization stand that kind of scrutiny these days?" When the man didn't answer, he sensed he'd struck a chord. "Way I hear it, you can't afford a distraction either. Not with Ramirez and Daily both itching to dismantle your operation and divide it up between them."

Tomsino's eyes narrowed. "What do you know about Ramirez and Daily?"

Folding his arms over his chest, Lucky leaned one shoulder against the doorjamb. The night air was cool but his skin was feverish, lit by a deadly grimness. "Word's on the street. You've already got your hands full. You don't need this kind of complication."

"You're the one complicating things, Boucher. And you've made an unfortunate choice." The smile the man gave him was as sharp as a blade. "Tell the lady I'll be back."

Lucky watched until the limo had pulled away before he stepped back inside the house. He locked the door and made his way upstairs, with the man's parting words echoing and re-echoing in his head. Tomsino didn't make idle threats. He didn't have to. There wasn't a doubt in his mind that Jacey hadn't seen the last of him. And he wasn't quite sure yet just what he was going to do about that.

"Lucky?" Her drowsy voice held a note of uncertainty as he entered the bedroom. "I thought you'd left."

"*Non*. I'm here, *Boo*." He dropped his pants and slipped back into bed, sliding his arms around her warm form.

She wrapped her arms around his waist and shivered. "You're cold. Where'd you go?"

"Out of my mind, with you, a little while ago." Seeking to distract her, he brushed her mouth with hers. "Take me there again."

But she reared back, studying his face in the shadows. "Lucky?"

He released a breath, sensing the inevitability of the upcoming scene. "You had a visitor."

"At this hour? Who was it?"

"Tomsino."

That news had brought her fully awake. He could feel it in the taut stillness of her body against his. "Wanting to continue our earlier conversation, no doubt."

"He'll be back." He didn't fool himself that he'd done anything but delayed the unavoidable. But there were always ways out of any situation. He just needed time and cunning to think of the escape clause in this one.

"You're right, he will be back. And when he is, you need to let me talk to him."

It was that exact tone in her voice, he thought grimly, that exact thought that he'd wanted to avoid. "We discussed this earlier. I'll handle Tomsino."

"Actually, you talked, but you didn't do a whole lot of listening. I think both are required to qualify it as a discussion. Lucky, think about it." She faced him in the near darkness, her head propped on her hand. "I've considered it and I'm still glad I all but told him to go to hell. I think it makes things look more realistic when I eventually agree to cooperate. It's the only option that will allow us to continue our investigation."

There was admiration coursing through him, even as he rejected her proposal. "I know what you're thinkin'. But you can't string along a man like that. It's too dangerous. I'm not going to let him get within ten yards of you."

She sat up in bed, the sheet falling to her waist. "You

don't allow me to do anything, remember? I make my own choices."

The sliver of moonlight slanted across her chest, gilding one breast, leaving the other in shadow. Because he found the sight too distracting, he tugged the sheet up and tucked the edge beneath her arm. "It's a dangerous game you're suggestin', with an equally dangerous man. We could try to run an endplay around him, only to find ourselves caught in our own trap."

"You have a devious mind. You'll think of something." The quiet certainty in her voice stunned him, and sent a tide of warmth coursing through his chest. "In the meantime, we have to protect the integrity of the case. I can't fail J. Walter. This development just shows how high the stakes really are for him."

"Tomsino won't be easy to fool," he said, acceptance spreading through him. He was past the stage of rejecting, violently, the thought of her becoming embroiled with the man. She already was involved. Now he had to figure out a way around that. "I know him well enough to be certain of it."

"Yes, you said you knew him."

He waited tensely, but she didn't go on. The silence hummed and vibrated between them. And perhaps because she didn't demand answers, didn't even seem to expect them, he found himself offering her some. "I've worked plenty of jobs since leavin' the bayou. Some didn't pay enough to make rent. The ones that paid better required a certain...willingness to overlook legal niceties." If he was skirting wide of the truth of the matter, it was habit. But he didn't doubt that she read between the wide lines of what he wasn't saying.

He rolled to his side, tried to see her eyes. He wanted to watch her expression when he said what he had to say. "I'd worked for small-timers before, low level wise guys, but Tomsino is several cuts above them, at least in terms of the size of his operation and his success."

"Why did you decide to leave him?"

Her question hung in the air, circling close to the one thing he didn't want to reveal to her at all. He'd still been working for Tomsino when his *cousine* Luella had given his name to Charlotte Wheeler after she'd asked for the name of a man who got results and wasn't all that concerned about who he hurt in the process.

"I've never been an angel, but when you balance long enough on the edge between good and bad, it's only a matter of time before somethin' nudges you over to one side or the other." It had been a long long time -before he'd realized that by sticking with Wheeler and Associates and getting his license, he'd leaped free of that tightwire. He didn't recall having made a conscious choice at all. It was just something that had happened.

"You didn't have a record. Not even a traffic ticket. And believe me, I checked." Her tone was wry. "Of course, I didn't exactly find any merit badges, either."

He'd known she would have run a check, of course. In her line of work, it was a given. But it pleased him nonetheless. Even then, Jacey had been thorough and meticulous in her work. "I was no Boy Scout, but it wasn't for lack of being prepared." He tugged on her hand and pulled her sideways, so she toppled on him. His arm came out to clasp her waist to hold her there.

But when his fingers roamed down to the sexy curve of her butt, she slapped a hand on his chest and straightened a little to look at him. "I have to contact J. Walter to let him know what's going on first thing in the morning."

His hand stilled. He knew she was right. But the resignation that accompanied the realization did nothing to dispel his very real concern for her safety. "I know."

"One of the Garveys is the connection to Tomsino." She settled herself more comfortably against his chest as she mused. "We'll have to follow that link to fully discredit that member of the family."

"Tomsino will be givin' you part of that information the next time he contacts you."

She nodded. "Running a double investigation is going to require contracting with more outside operatives than usual. Tomsino will be watching us, but he won't know what the other employees are up to. Hopefully that will help us take him by surprise."

"Lianna Wharton was the first to come to you, so it's obvious she had the same information as Tomsino regarding the old man's health and your involvement. We already know about her son's drug background. That in itself could be the link. Maybe he was somehow working for Tomsino while he was in college." Although Lucky had never been involved in that aspect of the man's operation, he knew he was a major supplier in the area. "The kid might even be hooked himself, and Tomsino got to his mother through blackmail or the promise of treatment, or somethin'."

"She could afford treatment for him, and from my brief meeting, I'd say blackmail is more his style. He didn't come off as very altruistic."

That was an understatement. "Then there's Stephen. A stockbroker could be pretty useful to a guy who has money to launder. Wonder if we could get our hands on his client list."

It didn't seem strange at all to be holding a beautiful naked woman in his arms and be discussing investigative techniques. Which should be enough to scare the hell out of him.

"Given Amanda's history with men, she might be an easy mark for someone like Tomsino, too." The possibilities there were endless. "Even Rupert could be used, either because of fear for one of his children, or because of an indiscretion of his own."

Jacey raised herself up on one elbow. "So basically, the only Garvey we haven't incriminated yet is Mark."

"Give us time, darlin'." Her position drew the hollow of her collarbone into sharp relief, and his lips went to explore it.

"I'm not sure how much time we have left. What day is it?"

"Tuesday. No, wait. Wednesday."

"We just got a break. Wednesday mornings are trash pickup days in Mark Garvey's neighborhood. I discovered that when I called a Realtor with a house for sale in the area."

"*Oui,* that is incredible good fortune." Irony was rife in his voice. "Given the choice between makin' love and wadin' through someone's trash, I would choose Dumpster-divin', everytime."

Her hand slid down his chest, a long smooth stroke, and then lingered lower. "How about if I promise to let you wash my back after we're done?"

"Never let it be said that I refused to compromise." She bounded from the bed with a bit more eagerness than he would expect, given the chore they had before them. Lucky followed more slowly. He knew she was jazzed by the thought of beginning her plan for double-crossing Tomsino, no matter how small the start. He was reluctant to reveal the worry that was growing in his gut.

They still had to find a way to accomplish the task and live long enough to tell about it.

Chapter 11

Jacey had left Lucky to the unenviable task of sorting through Mark Garvey's garbage while she'd gotten dressed and gone in to the office. She'd wanted to set up the meeting with J. Walter as soon as possible. That didn't mean, however, that she hadn't taken the time to follow through on her promise to Lucky. A smile curved her lips as she thought of their interlude in the shower. She'd always believed in keeping her word, but rarely was such virtue so well-rewarded.

She waited until getting to the office to call Garvey on a secure cell phone she kept there. After setting up a meeting time for an hour later, she went to the rental agency and exchanged her rental car. She picked J. Walter up on the corner of the block where his building was located.

The man got into the car and after a terse greeting,

strapped himself in. "What's this new development you indicated on the phone? Sounded like trouble to me."

"Well, it's a complication." Jacey checked for traffic before pulling away from the curb. She filled him in on the latest developments, including having Tomsino approach her with his demand.

When she'd finished, the older man cursed, then immediately apologized. She shook her head. "You don't have to worry about offending me. Believe me, I've thought worse since my meeting with him."

"From the sounds of him, he's no different from any number of thugs I've met over the years, trying to muscle in on someone else's hard work." He gave her a sharp look from beneath white bristly brows. "Slapping fancy suits and titles on those guys doesn't make them any better than this Tomsino you're talking about. I know the type."

She slowed, turned the corner. "I'm sure you do. And you're right, he's a thug. But I have it on very good authority that he's a dangerous one. I have a plan in mind for how to proceed, but I needed to check with you first to get your input. He's obviously got some connection to a member of your family, and is hoping to parlay that into influence in your company."

"I'll see him in hell first," J. Walter vowed grimly.

Jacey almost smiled. The man was a warrior, through and through. She'd been concerned when she first noticed him striding toward the car. Just in the short time since they'd begun their association, he had failed, physically. His suit hung more loosely on his tall frame, and strain was evident on his features.

This latest development wouldn't help his stress level.

"I didn't expect you to roll over for this guy. But you deserve to know what your options are. If you feel that continuing to retain my services in any way compromises this investigation, you need to tell me now."

His frown was fiercely impatient. "Don't be ridiculous. It wouldn't matter which agency I used. The man obviously thinks he can bully anyone into submission."

She nodded. "I think so, too. He'll contact me again, and I plan to allow him to think that he's succeeded. I'll tell him I'm preparing dual reports, one with the actual results of the investigation, and another for you, sanitized per his specifications. This allows me to continue my investigation for you, while gathering evidence that will connect one of your relatives to Tomsino."

J. Walter was silent long enough to have her glancing over at him. "I don't like it," he finally said. "What's the fallout for you when my will designates someone else as the one chosen to run the company? I'll be gone, but you'll still be here and the man is going to know, or at least suspect, that you double-crossed him."

"Don't worry about it." She wasn't going to admit that she hadn't quite figured out that aspect of the plan yet. But she had every confidence that she and Lucky would come up with something. "I just want to assure you that the investigation won't be compromised. But if you would feel safer starting over with a fresh company, that might buy you some time from the man."

He heaved a sigh. "Time is one thing I don't have, Ms. Wheeler. And not knowing how the man learned of our association makes it near impossible to guarantee he wouldn't discover if I hired another. No, what you're suggesting is right up my alley. Double-crossing the bastard and beating him at his own game. But you haven't convinced me that you won't be putting yourself in danger by doing so. Charlotte would never let me rest easy in my grave if something happened to you while you worked a case for me."

Mention of her mother gave her a little jolt. With a dart of guilt she realized she hadn't spoken to her since the night of Peter's engagement party. She'd dreaded having another encounter with her over Lucky, especially in light of the recent changes in their relationship.

With effort, she pushed the thought from her mind. She'd contact her mother in the next couple of days, and if their conversation involved yet another disagreement, that wouldn't be unusual. Nothing was going to make her regret the change in the relationship between her and Lucky. She wasn't quite sure yet what the future held, but whatever it was would be between the two of them.

Checking the rearview mirror again, she said wryly, "You don't need to worry. That confidentiality clause precludes even my mother from the details of our association."

"She's a determined woman. You're a lot like her."

Her brows shot up. She wasn't sure how to interpret that remark. When the next opportunity arose she turned, headed back in the direction of his building.

He went on. "You've got her grit and her determination. More heart, though. That I'd say you got from your father. At any rate, I'm betting on you to be more than a match for Tomsino. I'll want to be kept apprised of events as they occur, as per our original agreement."

"You can count on it."

His next words then had her head swiveling toward

him. "If I begin to think at anytime, though, that this investigation is putting you and your operatives in too much danger, I reserve the right to pull the plug on the whole thing. I have enough on my conscience without that, as well."

There was nothing to be said to that, so she remained silent. But as she drove back to Garvey Enterprises, she was well aware that even if the assignment was pulled from her agency, that wouldn't necessarily protect them from Tomsino. The only way to do that was, as J. Walter had put it, to beat the man at his own game.

Jacey returned the rental car and headed back toward the office. She found Lucky already in when she got there and as she stood in the doorway of his office, her heart skittered a bit as she looked at him. He'd obviously gone home at some point. Although he hadn't bothered to shave, he was wearing yet another obnoxious T-shirt, this one announcing that P.I.s did it undercover. She shook her head and refused to comment on it.

Instead she strolled in, shutting the door behind her. Rounding his desk, she said, "So, am I going to lose you to the Sanitation Department anytime soon?"

He looked up from the sheaf of papers he was perusing. There was a glint in his eye when he saw her. "You owe me, big-time, for that."

"I'm almost certain I prepaid that particular account."

There was a thread of pure wickedness in his tone. "*Mais oui,* but I may need to renegotiate. Based on what I've discovered, you owe me much, much more."

Their teasing was abruptly forgotten. "You found something? What was it?"

"A couple things of interest. First of all was this." He opened a folder and withdrew a sheet of paper. Taking it from him, she saw that it was Mark Garvey's cell bill. There were some calls circled, twelve in all, to the same number. She checked the date. It was for the current month's payment.

"And do I have to guess whose number it is?"

"It's Tomsino's cell."

She was about to open her mouth to ask if he was sure, then closed it again. He'd arranged the call that had gotten the man away from the restaurant last night. Given their past relationship, it figured Lucky would have the man's number.

Studying the dates, she did some calculation. They started well before the time J. Walter had approached her about the case. "What is Tomsino into?"

Lucky lifted a shoulder. "What isn't he into? Drugs, prostitution, extortion, racketeerin', loan-sharkin'…he considers himself well diversified."

She leaned against the corner of his desk facing him, the bill still in her hand. "This is a start, anyway. Involvement in any one of those activities would provide Tomsino with blackmail opportunities. Do you think this is enough to start heavy surveillance on him?"

"It's only a matter of time until Tomsino contacts you again. He'll reveal which Garvey he wants sanitized then. If we have to, we can always switch our focus, but for now, this is enough for me."

She nodded. "It would help to get some of this in place before Tomsino realizes we know who his link is. That way we stay one step ahead of him." When she saw that Lucky's interest seemed to be arrowed on her legs, she made an effort to tug her skirt farther down over them. "What do you think about using two dozen operatives?"

He didn't seem to register her outlandish statement. "Hmm?" His hand came out to cup her calf, and at the firm kneading her temperature shot up ten degrees.

"I was thinking the pig and the cow could drive the first car and we could fill the other with the chickens."

His tone was distracted. "Good thinkin'." He stroked a hand up her leg to her thigh, only to have it slapped away. He looked up with a wounded expression on his face. "What? I was listenin'. More operatives. We'll need them for the covert surveillance."

"And you just agreed to get them off the nearest farm. Now pay attention." To make sure he did, she circled the desk and sat in a chair opposite him. "I'd like to place a GPS surveillance device on his car now, today, before Tomsino catches up with me again. Neither of us will be able to be involved in the actual surveillance since Garvey knows me, and Tomsino would recognize both of us. But we can track the GPS device from the computer here, and communicate with the teams by cell phone."

"Six operatives, three male-female teams." A male-female combination generally aroused far less suspicion than would two males. Lucky's attention was firmly back on business. He snuck another peek at Jacey's legs. Almost firmly. "Which agency are you going with?"

"I think SVS Laboratories. I've used their operatives before, and many of them are the right age. Middle-aged couples in the cars attract less attention."

"LRE Services has the best equipment," he reminded her.

"We can supplement wherever they're short. At any rate, it may come down to who has operatives free to begin immediately. Do you want to make the contact?"

He looked at her, his expression shrewd. "Why? What are you going to do?"

"Put the GPS device in place before Garvey leaves work."

Lucky nodded. "I'll get operatives over here and brief them. Better make a list now of the equipment they're going to require. That might take the longest time, getting everything rounded up." He went to the desk and sat down, taking out a pencil and pen. "Rental cars, plain sedans. Cell phones with car chargers."

"With rentals it works best if they bring double cigarette lighter plugs so they can be constantly recharging their cell phones."

"Extra phone batteries," Lucky noted, jotting everything down. "High-powered binoculars."

"I'll take care of getting photos for them of Mark and Tomsino for identification," Jacey promised. "Each team should have a small digital video recorder with zoom and a digital camera with a zoom lens and a large-capacity chip. I want pictures of Mark Garvey and anyone he's with."

"They should probably have a good 35 mm with zoom then," Lucky said, without looking up. "Identification is going to be essential on this."

"Extra batteries for everything," she added, rising to pace. Now that action was near, adrenaline was beginning to course through her. "A laptop so they can download any pictures or video clips right away and burn the DVDs right there."

"It'd probably be safest to have them go to a twenty-four-hour photo shop and e-mail any pictures to our server at the end of each shift."

She nodded, still thinking. The GPS device would help ensure that they could always locate Mark's vehicle even if the operatives lost him. But the team of agents would become imperative when it became time to follow the man on foot.

The ring of her cell interrupted her, and she took it from the pocket of her ivory suit jacket and answered it. At the sound of the voice on the other end of the line, her pulse quickened.

The conversation was brief, and throughout it she was aware of Lucky's interested gaze on her. When she was finished, she flipped the phone shut with a feeling of excitement. "That was my contact in the FTC. When she was digging around for information on Stephen Garvey's file from a couple years ago she stumbled on something else. The FTC didn't drop the investigation when they didn't make the case then. They continued it, covertly, to gather more evidence." She knew the sudden look of interest on his face was reflected on her own. "She couldn't tell me much, but she thinks an arrest is imminent."

"I knew that the guy workin' the desk was a helluva lot more than a security guard."

"Meaning?"

"He's a cop of some sort. Could be federal, I suppose." When she tilted her head quizzically, he shrugged. "You spend enough time dodgin' them, gets to where you can recognize the type."

"I'll have to take your word on that. I suppose it's

possible the FTC have some sort of law-enforcement agent inside as part of their investigation."

"That's one Garvey grandchild we won't have to worry about investigatin'," Lucky observed.

"I'm starting to feel badly for J. Walter." The man truly hadn't been fortunate in his relatives. "Mark's ex-wife seemed to think quite of bit of Stephen. I was hoping he might turn out to be the one we could recommend as J. Walter's replacement."

"Somethin' tells me the old guy won't be too willin' to have someone runnin' the company from behind bars."

"Suspecting what we do about Mark's involvement with Tomsino and Jeffrey's past drug dealing, the prospects are getting limited." She sighed, then rose. "I'll meet you back here after I finish planting the device. Hopefully we can line up operatives that quickly."

"Leave it to me." He stood and rounded the desk, blocking her path. "But leave somethin' else with me, before you go." He tugged on her hand and she went willingly into his arms. His mouth covered hers and sparks sizzled along her nerve endings. When he raised his head, his eyes, those dark wicked eyes, were gleaming at her. "Last night was cut short, *n'est ce pas?*"

She indulged herself a moment longer by hooking her arms around his neck. "That's the nice thing about nights. The end of every day brings another."

A strand of hair had escaped from the intricate knot she'd arranged it in. He reached up and brushed it back, the gesture oddly tender. "Is that an offer?"

She caressed his nape with her fingertips. "I'm not sure I should say. My propositions have a way of scaring you off."

His expression was pure sin. "I'm not runnin', darlin', so you better get used to the fact that you'll be havin' some company again tonight."

Going on tiptoe, she gave him a lingering kiss, one that threatened her insides with combustion. "I'm glad you stopped running. Because I don't think I ever told you that I was a pretty good sprinter in high school."

"Really?" He looked intrigued. "I've always admired athletic females. All that...bouncin'."

Because her lips wanted, badly, to curve, she firmed them. Dropping her hands she stepped back. "You have a one-track mind, Boucher."

"*Mais oui.* And tonight you'll be the only thing on it." With the promise in his voice still ringing in her ears, Jacey went back to her office on legs that were inclined to wobble slightly.

The doorbell rang. Smiling, Jacey put down her pen and looked at her watch. Lucky had called and said he had business to attend to before he stopped over. He must have finished earlier than he had expected. Rising, she strode to the door. The anticipation that was curling inside her was at once pleasant and alarming. It wouldn't do to allow herself to think of him as a permanent fixture in her life, at least outside the office. Although they hadn't discussed it since their relationship had changed, it was important to both of them that their friendship remain unaltered once they were no longer lovers. She'd assured him at the beginning that that wouldn't be a problem, but at the moment, she couldn't think of a single one of her admittedly limited lovers with whom she was still in contact.

But that was different, she told herself firmly. None of those men had been friends as well as lovers. None of them had been Lucky.

She gave a cursory look out the peephole, and then froze. Her breath strangled in her lungs as anticipation withered, to be replaced with trepidation. The man standing on her front porch was none other than Vinny Tomsino.

Swallowing hard, she thought quickly. Backtracking, she went to her desk and took a mini tape recorder from the drawer. A tape was already installed, so she pressed rewind. Dashing to the bedroom, she replaced the sheer robe she was wearing with a more bulky terry-cloth one. The doorbell rang again. She pressed Record, and dropped the recorder into the pocket of her robe. Then she went to the door and unlocked it, pulled it open.

"Ms. Wheeler." The man's smile was unpleasant. "You and I have some unfinished business."

Looking beyond him, she saw a long black limo parked illegally in front of her home. "You're a pushy man, Mr. Tomsino." She glanced back at him grimly. "I don't like to be pushed."

"No one does, but it gets results. I don't want to discuss business standing outside."

She surveyed him stonily. "And I don't want you in my home."

In answer, he slammed the flat of his hand against the door, forcing her to step back to avoid having it hit her. He stepped inside, closed the door behind him. "Like I said, the porch is no place to talk business."

He walked by her to the living room, stood looking around. Her stomach jittered. She didn't want him here.

Didn't even want the memory of his presence tainting her home. He'd lost the phony civil demeanor he'd donned for the meeting in the restaurant. He'd determined to get exactly what he wanted, and Jacey knew intuitively that he would do whatever it took to accomplish that end.

"Where's Boucher?"

She lifted a shoulder, watched him roam the room. "Not here yet." She saw him send a glance toward the stairway and felt a cold chill go down her spine. Her laptop was set up in a spare bedroom she used as an office, tracking the GPS device she'd planted on Mark Garvey's car. "Does he really seem the type to hide upstairs and let a woman handle something like this?"

He looked back at her then and smirked. "No. He is the type to be found in a woman's bedroom, though. Must be in another broad's tonight, huh? What's the matter? Did he lose interest already?"

The taunt burned, perhaps because there was just enough truth in it to sting. Not that she suspected Lucky was with someone else. He wouldn't be dishonest in a relationship. But she knew him well enough to realize that he wasn't the type to stay in one long-term, either.

The reminder made her voice sharp. "You're a persistent man, Mr. Tomsino. Most would have considered my refusal the other night as final."

He straightened his suit jacket and seated himself on the couch. This evening he was outfitted in a navy pinstripe that should have made him look like a banker. But bankers didn't wear that mask of utter ruthlessness. "No answer is final until it's the one I want. And yours wasn't the one I wanted. Before I leave, it will be."

The scene had to progress much as the man anticipated. That was the only way to protect the integrity of the investigation. But she had a role to play and she stuck to it. He wouldn't expect her to capitulate easily. Which was fortunate, because that meant in the end, she really wasn't being called on to pretend much at all.

"Nothing is going to change my mind." She didn't sit down. She didn't want to get that close to him. In a gesture of defiance, she jammed her hands in the pocket of her robe, all too aware of the recorder in there. "I didn't build my business by caving in any time a small-time hood made some demands."

He said nothing at that. He didn't have to. The animosity shimmered off him in waves. "You want to be real careful. Your cooperation is a given. At least, if you want to keep Boucher alive." He shrugged, a small smile settling on his lips. "That's the deal. You give me what I want and he gets to breathe a while longer. It's a rough city. Lots of things can happen."

Icicles of fear speared through her. Even knowing that the reaction was exactly the one he wanted couldn't help her control it. She'd known he'd come armed with threats. She'd expected no less. But she'd assumed they'd be aimed at her. She'd been prepared for that.

She was certain the man would be only too happy to follow through on this threat. There was something in his voice whenever he mentioned Lucky. There was bad blood between them, maybe because Lucky had walked away from his organization.

"Nothing to say?" His smile grew unpleasant.

She hugged her arms around her waist and bit her lip, her response not totally feigned. Real fear was coursing through her. "I'm the owner of the company, and I'm the one who makes the decisions about the investigations. This has nothing to do with him."

"I think it does. Sit down."

Swallowing hard, she chose the chair farthest from him and sank into it.

His eyes held a gleam of satisfaction. "Now that you're ready to listen, I'll tell you what you're going to do. You'll continue the assignment old man Garvey hired you for, but the reports you make will make it clear that Mark Garvey is the only family member fit to take over the old man's business. Have you told him about our talks?"

"No," she lied. "I just updated him today, but didn't mention it. I didn't want him to take the assignment to another company."

Tomsino looked pleased. "Good. Because if he pulls the job from you and I have to start over with someone else, I won't be happy. With me unhappy, things won't be healthy for your lover."

"It's not going to be as easy as you think." She manufactured a tremor for her voice. "To make it appear legitimate, I have to continue my investigation. I'll need to find evidence proving the other three grandchildren unfit, as well as continuing to look into Mark Garvey's background. I can't be sure that mine is the only company J. Walter contracted with. Sometimes a client will hire two to work independently of each other and compare the results. Money certainly would be no object for him."

"He hasn't hired anyone else," the man said surely. Jacey's interest piqued. How the heck did he know that? And how had he found out about him hiring her agency?

"Focus all you want on the other three, but Mark is off-limits. The old man isn't going to know the difference whether you make up the reports or actually follow through on the investigation."

Mentally she congratulated herself for the accuracy of their guess about Tomsino's connection in the Garvey family. Now all they had to discover through the surveillance teams was what hold Tomsino had over Mark Garvey.

She decided to be straightforward about her interest. "Why are you so interested in having Mark at the helm of Garvey Enterprises? What's his association with you?"

Tomsino gave her a wink. The jovial gesture on that menacing face was oddly repulsive. "Let's just say, it's in my best interests to have him there. That's all you need to know." He slapped his hands on his knees and rose with some difficulty. Taking his cell phone out of his suit pocket he asked, "What's your cell number?"

Reluctantly, she recited it for him.

"I'll contact you for regular updates. Are you doing written reports for the old man?"

"Of course." In truth, she never would have considered it. Putting things in writing was far too risky, as evidenced by the information that already somehow landed in Tomsino's hands. With the explosion of technology, there were far more secure ways to share details, if the reports needed to be documented.

He nodded, headed toward the door. Now that he'd gotten what he'd come for, he appeared eager to be gone. "Get me copies of everything you've shared so far with the old man, and anything else you prepare for him."

Satisfaction laced through her. He'd get copies all right. But they would be copies that contained phony information. She followed him as far as the hallway, waited impatiently for him to go. But she wasn't prepared for him to turn from the door suddenly and reach for her.

"Take your hands off me," she warned in a deadly tone. Her defense training might not be enough to help her get the better of the man, but the urge to find out was coursing through her, searing through caution. His fingers were wrapped so tightly around her wrist she could feel bone grinding on bone. Her skin crawled beneath his touch.

"Don't worry." His tone was insulting. "I'm not interested in Boucher's leavings. You play by my rules and nobody will get hurt. Make sure you keep your boyfriend from doing anything stupid." He dropped her hand and walked to the door.

The moment it closed behind him she locked it. Then reaction slammed into her and she let out a shaky breath, felt her knees weaken. She was swamped with an overwhelming need to shower, to scrub the feel of him from her flesh.

Lifting her wrist to examine it, she saw it was already red, the outline of his fingers showing clearly. It would bruise, and she knew the mark was meant as a warning to Lucky. Tomsino was attempting to use each of them to keep the other in line. Knowing his ploy didn't detract from its effectiveness.

Finally remembering the tape recorder in her pocket, she took it out, turned it off. At least now she had some evidence of Tomsino's involvement, and the threats he

made. But even as she had the thought, she realized it
was going to take far more than a record of their conversation to ensure Lucky's safety.

Chapter 12

The alley was dark, and smelled of stale urine and cheap wine. There was an occasional rustle of rats foraging for food. Lucky figured it was a fitting enough location for the meeting he'd arranged.

The environment didn't seem all that foreign to him. The days when he'd spent all too much time in places identical to this one seemed only too recent.

There was a sound at the entrance and every muscle in his body tensed. This was a dangerous gamble, one that could backfire easily. But it was the best plan he could devise for outwitting Tomsino. It wouldn't be enough to double-cross the man. To make sure he didn't come after them when it was over, they had to take him down.

The people he was meeting tonight would be tools to that end. If they showed. And if they agreed.

A shadow loomed, then a figure stepped into the alley. "Boucher?"

Lucky recognized the voice. Enrico Ramirez was the first on the scene. "I'm here." He stepped closer, saw the man had come with two of his bodyguards. He'd expected nothing less. Raising his hands, he submitted to the pat-down without a word. He felt the guard's hands pause when they found the weapon strapped to his ankle.

"Knife," the guard reported.

"Leave it," Lucky advised. But the man waited for some unseen signal from Ramirez before he did just that and rose.

"Check the rest of the alley." Ramirez had the wheezy breathless voice of the chronic asthmatic. Rumor had it that he carried an inhaler in one pocket and a Glock in the other.

The two men came back in moments. "Nothing here."

Ramirez nodded. "Okay, Boucher, let's hear what you've got."

"Not yet," he responded. "I told you, you're not the only one invited to this party. Let's wait for our other guest."

As if on cue, a late-model silver sedan drove slowly by. Moments later, it pulled over, and footsteps approached the alley. Daily had arrived.

The man appeared, flanked by three others, and Lucky was struck by the contrast between Tomsino's two foes. Daily was tall, broad and blond, while Ramirez was short, wiry and swarthy. But they were two of a kind for all that. They both made their living on the wrong side of the law, and they were united in their hatred of Tomsino.

The earlier scene was re-enacted as Daily ordered his guards to frisk Lucky. There was a short tussle when it became apparent neither Ramirez nor Daily was going to submit to a search by the other man's bodyguards.

"Why don't I do the honors?" Lucky suggested, as tempers flared. Grudgingly each man agreed, and he performed the act briskly. "Ramirez is carryin' a piece and Daily's got a knife," he announced, rising. "Do we want to dance here all night, or are we goin' to give up our weapons for the duration of the meetin'?"

There was silence, long enough for worry to begin gnawing before each man gave up their weapon to their respective bodyguards. It was with more than a little trepidation that Lucky handed his knife to Ramirez's guard. All his instincts were honed rapier-sharp.

When the guards had all withdrawn the two men turned as one and Daily spoke. "Let's get to the business that brought us here. You got five minutes, Boucher."

"We're all here because we have one thing in common. Each of our lives would improve if Vinny Tomsino weren't in it."

He'd said as much to the men when he'd called them earlier to set up this meeting. And they were interested. Their presence tonight attested to that. Whether they were interested enough to put aside their distrust of each other, and of him, remained to be seen.

"I have a plan to get rid of Tomsino." Lucky leaned a shoulder against the next-door building facing the two men. With his back to the dead end of the alley, and the other two at its mouth, his was the most precarious position. "But in order for it to work, I need to have him distracted, his resources divided. From what I understand, neither of you has a big enough organization to take him on alone. What I'm suggestin' is that you join forces, at least for the moment."

"Why the hell should we do that?" It was Daily speaking. His voice sounded like it came from a gravel truck.

"With Tomsino out of the way, the two of you could split up his territory and his operations. Both of you stand to gain a great deal."

"And what do you stand to gain?" Ramirez wheezed.

"I stay alive. An important detail for me. I don't care about a share of whatever you take from Tomsino in the course of this whole thing. You can divide everythin' between yourselves. I'm offerin' to give you information about his deliveries, his payoffs, schedules, locations of his operations…whatever details I get will be turned over to you. And you two take it from there. But I need you to act fast, hit hard and often."

"I don't like it," Daily said. But he was intrigued. Lucky didn't have to be able to see his face to know that. "How do we know this isn't a setup by Tomsino to take us both out?"

His voice patient, Lucky said, "It's not like you'll be carrying out the attacks yourselves. You send some of your men to take care of a delivery and something goes bad, how does that affect you?"

"I'm in," Ramirez interjected. "I can handle this on my own, though. I don't need no help."

"That's up to Daily. If he's not interested in partnerin' with you for this operation, it's yours." Lucky hoped it wouldn't come to that. Greed was getting in the way of any good sense Ramirez might have possessed. He doubted he had the manpower to carry this thing off without help.

"If he's in, so am I." The response, although grudging, relieved something inside Lucky. "But we need details and time to plan how we're going to pull anything like this off."

"I can help you with that." Lucky reached inside his jacket, then stilled when he saw the other two tense. "Relax." He pulled out some folded papers and smoothed them out. "I've got some details here, and I even did a little of the plannin' for you."

"You're later than you thought you'd be." After letting him in, Jacey followed Lucky from the hallway to the living room. "You missed Tomsino."

He whirled so quickly then she almost ran into him. "He stopped by here tonight?"

Her wrist throbbed, as if in response. "He was here. It's Mark Garvey, Lucky. I didn't get a clue as to what the connection was, but he's the one Tomsino wants sanitized."

A grim mask had descended over his features. "What did he say? Did he threaten you?"

A shiver snaked down her spine at the menace in his voice. At that moment, she would have bet that Lucky and Tomsino were evenly matched when it came to sheer danger. "He threatened *you*. He said you'd be killed if I didn't cooperate."

To her dismay, he nodded, as if in satisfaction. "Good. That tells me he's thinkin' twice about harmin' you. Your family is too high-profile in the city for the likes of him to take on."

His casual dismissal of the threats fired the concern that had been gnawing at her all night. "Don't dismiss it so easily. I had the impression that he would be only too happy to get rid of you."

"Don' worry, *cher.*" He came closer and took her shoulders in his hands, brought her close to him. Resting his chin in her hair, he murmured, "He thinks he has you scared for me, and that will make him feel invincible. He'll be less likely to see what's comin' at him until he's been hit."

"What exactly is coming at him? What were you doing tonight?"

"Arrangin' for Tomsino to be distracted. With his attention on a dozen different things goin' wrong at once, he'll have less time to focus on what we're up to." He gave her a brief, and she was sure, very abbreviated version of his evening.

Frost slicked up her spine. "Given their occupations, those two men are probably little better than Tomsino. You took a huge risk meeting with them both tonight." The nonchalant shrug he gave infuriated her. "You should have discussed it with me first, Lucky. This is my case. We assess the risks together. How do we even know this will work? Maybe we ought to take what we have to the police."

"The police?" His tone was derisive. "And tell them what, darlin'? That mean ol' Tomsino said bad things to you, threatened my life? How you goin' to prove that?"

"With this." She reached into the pocket of her robe and pulled out the mini-recorder. With a push of a button she replayed a portion of the tape for him before shutting it off again.

A delighted smile crossed his lips and he picked up her hand, kissed the palm. "That's my brainy lady. But you took a risk, and it really wasn't worth it. He could have discovered what you were doin', and there's no tellin' what he would have done. He's a nasty bastard."

She didn't need the reminder. "What do you mean, it wasn't worth the risk? It's evidence."

"It might interest the police if they tripped over my body and needed an idea who to look at, but right now this would be worthless to them." Cupping her shoulders in his hands, he kneaded them gently, his gaze steady on hers. "Trust me. This is the best way. The only way I can think of."

She looked away. She wasn't so sure, but at the moment she had nothing better to offer. "How do you know what details to give those men? He's bound to have changed his operation since you worked for him."

"But my friend worked for him as recently as a few days ago." And Remy, he remembered, hadn't hesitated to tell him everything when Lucky had called him this afternoon. That kind of unselfishness had nearly unmanned him. By giving Lucky the information that could dismantle Tomsino's operation, he'd ensured there would be no job for him to return to.

And if his plan failed, there was a good chance that Tomsino would start looking hard for the source of the leaks. It wasn't only Jacey and Lucky's lives that might hang in the balance here. It could well be Remy's, too.

A bolt of determination tightened through him. He was humbled by the risk his friend had taken without question. And Remy's involvement just raised the stakes. He wouldn't fail. He couldn't.

"I still don't like it."

There was a little frown on her brow, the one she always got when she was trying to puzzle something out. "Whether you want to or not, there's going to be a time when the police will have to get involved. If we find evidence that will nail Tomsino during the course of this investigation, we'd be better off letting law enforcement handle it."

"T'es bien." He kissed her forehead. "That's right. But that time isn't now. I just set the plan in motion, darlin'. We have to give it some time for things to start happenin'."

He could feel her muscles relax beneath his fingers, a fraction at a time, so he brought her closer, rubbed his hand in slow circular motions at the base of her spine. She arched into him like a cat.

"How will we know when the time is right to act?"

He began walking backwards, urging her to the staircase that would take them to her bedroom. To heaven. "It's like bein' a demolitions expert, *mon ange.* Tonight I sprinkled the minefield. All we have to do is wait for the detonation."

The next day seemed to crawl by, although there was plenty to keep them busy. She and Lucky took turns monitoring the laptop and keeping in contact with the surveillance agents. Two teams had followed Mark Garvey to a restaurant the night before, where he'd met a woman for dinner, then Mark had proceeded later alone to a nightclub, where he'd stayed until 2:00 a.m. before going home. Photos had been taken of the woman he'd dined with, as well as the locations where he'd spent time.

One team had followed his companion home and

Jacey was digging up her identity now, based on the address. Hours of poring over property transfers had paid off when she was able to put a name to the face. Imelda Braun. The name wasn't familiar. She ran a NEXIS on her, figuring it would probably be a dead end. From what Garvey's neighbor had said, the man had a revolving door for a social life. She'd been surprised he'd gone home alone.

Lucky walked in to her office at the end of the day, a smug expression on his face. "What did you find out about the mystery lady last night?"

Removing her glasses, she rubbed her aching eyes. They'd overslept that morning and she hadn't had time to put her contacts in. "Nothing of interest. She's a public relations consultant in a large firm downtown. If she's mixed up in whatever Mark Garvey is, I haven't found evidence of it yet."

He made a commiserating noise. "Too bad. I didn't have much luck either." She leaned back in her chair, eyeing him speculatively. "I checked into the ownership of the restaurant and nightclub. Interesting how difficult it was to discover the owner of the club. Had to hire a forensic accountant to get through the blind alleys in the trail."

A feeling of anticipation hummed through her. "Who is it?"

He gave her a satisfied smile. "Name on the deed is Greta Barlow. She just happens to be Vinny Tomsino's sister."

She jumped up to give him a high five. "Why do I have a feeling we're getting close?"

"Because you're blindly optimistic?" But he had a

difficult time containing his own satisfaction as he took out his cell and pressed a number on its speed dial.

When his friend answered, he wasted no time in pleasantries. "The Golden Goose. What do you know about it?"

Remy's voice was amused. "Hello to you, too. You call more often than my *grand-mère*. She has much better telephone manners, by the way."

"It's Tomsino's, isn't it? He's got a blind deed to cover him, but he's the money behind it."

"It belongs to someone in his family. I don't know if I ever heard who. It doesn't matter. He uses it like his own."

"For what? Money launderin'? Drugs?"

A shrug sounded in the man's words. "Maybe all of those. Couldn't say. Only thing I know is that's one of the places the Round Table meets."

Impatience filled him. "Round Table? What's that?"

"High stakes gamblin', *mon ami*. Too rich for our blood. I heard the entry fee each night is ten thousand. They have games three nights a week, but change the locations around."

"Where are some other places they meet?"

Remy thought for a moment. "There's a restaurant called Morgan's. Sometimes it's there, after hours. Other times it's been at Chauncey's, a high-class strip joint on LaSalle. And I think I remember hearin' that it's sometimes held at Festina's, an after-hours club. Tomsino's got his fingers in all those places, although it's doubtful his name is on any of the deeds."

"Doesn't matter," Lucky said, his mind racing furiously. "It took less than eight hours for my guy to discover who owned the Golden Goose. Tomsino covered his tracks, but not well enough."

After disconnecting, he relayed the gist of the conversation to Jacey while making another call, this one to the forensic accountant he'd hired. He stopped in mid-explanation when the woman came on the line, and he gave her the names of the other businesses Remy had mentioned. After getting her promise to start work on them immediately, he ended the call and looked at Jacey.

Her cheeks flushed with excitement. "This could be it. Maybe Tomsino wants Mark at the helm of Garvey Enterprises to make sure the money doesn't run out. Or perhaps Mark owes him so much he thinks the only way he'll get it back is to place him in that position of power."

"We're a long way from provin' anythin'," he cautioned. The warning was as much for himself as for her. "But we have a good enough start that I think we deserve some special treatment this evenin'. A delicious meal in an intimate settin' would be a start."

He was pleased to see a flicker of regret on her face. "We can't go to a restaurant and still maintain contact with the surveillance teams."

"*Mais non.* But we can bring the restaurant to us, *n'est ce pas?*"

Candles flickered around the oversize claw-foot tub, their tiny tips of flame throwing dancing shadows on the walls. Jacey sat between Lucky's bent legs, leaning against his chest. She selected a piece of cheese from the plate balanced on his knee and tipped her head back to feed it to him. He brought their shared wineglass to her lips and she sipped.

Appetites of both sorts were satisfied, at least for the

moment. But her experience with this man had taught
her that the feeling would be momentary. Hunger sprang
easily and surprisingly often between them. She was
learning not to question it. Enjoying it was enough. At
least for now.

She held the loofah above his leg and squeezed,
watching the water run in little rivulets over his hair-
roughened skin. "When you think back, what was the
turning point in your life?" she asked thoughtfully.

He rubbed his face against the top of her head. "That
sounds like the kind of question that women ask and
men can never answer satisfactorily."

Her lips curved. "Mine was Richard Carter DeLong's
twenty-first birthday party."

"A party? Why?" His voice sounded close to her ear.
As soon as he spoke the words, he took her lobe in his
teeth to worry it.

She hunched a shoulder, but that didn't dissuade his
lips. "Richard was a childhood acquaintance my mother
pushed at me since I could walk. He was, is, the most
singularly boring and conceited man I've ever met. I
wasn't responding to his attentions that evening and my
mother dragged me aside to lecture me about it. I explained at great length that I didn't care about him or
his bank account or bloodline, all of which seemed to
impress her to no end. She wasn't hearing me. She very
rarely does. Finally, in desperation I told her I wasn't
interested in any of the young men in our circle. I didn't
want to marry someone based on their portfolio. I told
her I wanted what she and my father must have had."

The memory made her pensive, but it had long since
lost its power to sadden her. "Mother got this look of

real confusion on her face, and said, 'What in heaven's sakes are you talking about, Jacinda? Your father and I came from similar backgrounds and he was highly suitable. He was easily managed, as well, so I thought we'd match.'" She shook her head. "Her honesty shocked me, I suppose. But that's the moment I decided that whatever it took, I wasn't going to follow the path she tried to force on me."

He bent to kiss the skin on the back of her neck. "It's a leap from not becomin' your mother to gettin' a private investigator's license and chasin' after bad guys."

She shifted position so she could run the sponge over his chest. "Well, Mother and Richard DeLong had less to do with that than the collection of Nancy Drew books I secretly devoured when I was in grade school."

"Nancy Drew?" He began drawing pins out of her hair, and setting them on the side of the tub. "I've heard of her. Wasn't she a porn star in the eighties?"

She yanked on some chest hair and was gratified to hear him yelp. "She was a girl detective. I was reading wholesome material while you were hiding *Penthouse* under your mattress."

His smile sounded in his voice. "*Non.* My *grand-mère* would never have stood for that. And Sister Raymond would have forced me to kneel for hours while she prayed to Saint Jude for my soul's salvation. She did that often. It was quite tedious."

"Saint Jude?" A laugh bubbled out of her. "The patron saint of hopeless causes?"

"Sister Raymond had great faith. I didn't have the heart to tell her to give it up."

"Looking for a way to let the ladies down easy, even back then, hmm?"

Crooking a knuckle beneath her chin, he tilted her head back to cover her mouth with his. After a thorough kiss, he pulled away enough to murmur, "I'm not lookin' to let you down, *Boo*. I hope you believe that."

Her heart turned over. There was a tenderness beneath that tough and cocky facade that never failed to soften her insides to mush. And no matter what the future brought, she'd never regret having had him reveal that side to her.

The laptop glowed from its perch upon the countertop. The cell phone sat next to it. But neither item could draw their attention away from each other. Lucky reached over to set the wineglass and then the plate of food on the counter. Then he rose, taking her by both hands and drawing her up with him.

Stepping out of the tub he scooped her up and strode back to the bedroom without grabbing a towel. He laid her on top of the bed, and then followed her down to worship.

With meticulous care, he used his tongue to catch each tiny rivulet that streamed over her shoulders, her arms and breasts. Her fingers clutched his wet hair, and she thrilled at the pagan tattoo beat already beginning in her blood. She'd talked earlier of turning points. She was somehow certain that she'd chosen another one in her life when she'd taken Lucky as a lover. For better or worse, it was a choice she wasn't going to forget.

He slid down her body, his hands cupping her bottom and, before she realized his intention, he'd lifted her hips and pressed his mouth to the soft damp folds between her thighs.

Her breath left her lungs in a ragged rush and she gripped his shoulders, her nails biting into his skin. With every stroke of his tongue, sensitized nerve endings shuddered, then strained for the next peak. He entered her with one finger, and slowly drove her wild with the dual assault of hand and mouth.

The rest of the world spun away in a dizzying vortex that left only sensation crowding sensation, each layering over the other until every part of her system was screaming for release. Need whipped higher with every teasing dart of his tongue, with each probing touch. And hunger, so recently satisfied, roared to life and became a fever in her blood.

She tugged frantically at his shoulders, his name a moaning cry on her lips. It had to be now, right now and she wanted to feel him buried deep inside her. Wanted to feel one more time that rapid-fire build to screaming release, and know that he was with her every step of the way.

Lucky moved back up her body and she bucked insistently beneath him until he entered her with one violent surge of his hips that drove the breath from them both. Limbs tangled, their bodies lifted and met, over and over, hips slapping against hips as the pleasure spiraled, sparked higher with every movement. She clung to him, giving, demanding, meeting every violent thrust until he gave one last savage lunge and she crested, the moment spinning out for endless moments, drenching her in molten pleasure.

It was a long time before she was able to move again. Longer still before she wanted to. But eventually duty overcame lethargy and she rolled from the bed, slipping into a robe. While Lucky retrieved the laptop and cell, she extinguished the guttering candles and carried the plates and wine to the kitchen.

When the doorbell rang, her gaze flew to the clock. It was only eight, although it felt much later. She hesitated, though, her mind automatically flying to the last unannounced visitor she'd had.

A bolt of sheer foreboding twisted through her. Then her chin angled. Tomsino wouldn't be allowed to make her afraid to be in her own home. Still, as she crossed to the door, she snuck a look upstairs. It wouldn't be wise for Lucky to meet up with the man anytime soon. She couldn't predict his reaction, and from her conversation with Tomsino last night, it had become painfully clear that the loathing was mutual.

So it was actually with a feeling of relief that she identified her mother standing on her porch. Jacey pulled the door open, trying to remember the last time Charlotte had visited her here.

"Jacinda." Her mother's brows rose as she took in her dress. "It's rather early for you to retire for the evening, isn't it? Are you ill?"

"No." She suppressed the urge to secure her robe more tightly around herself. "I...I just got out of the tub. I'm afraid I'm not dressed for company."

"Well I'm not company, darling, I'm your mother. Aren't you going to invite me in?"

The thought of Lucky and Charlotte meeting here was little more appealing than if the visitor had turned out to be Tomsino after all.

"It's really not a good time, Mother."

"*Cher,* you took so long to return, I got lonely."

With a feeling of helplessness, Jacey turned at the sound of Lucky's voice. A moment later he appeared, stopping short in the hallway when he saw her at the door.

He had his jeans on, although the waistband was un-buttoned, and she sent up a silent prayer of thanks that he was at least partially clothed. She turned back to her mother's frozen expression and reached for composure. "As I said, Mother, it's not a good time."

"You bastard."

Jacey's jaw dropped. She'd never heard her mother utter even the mildest curse word, much less say one with such vehemence.

"Was this for my benefit? The most vile, revolting thing you could stoop to just to thumb your nose at me one more time?"

"Mother, stop!"

But Charlotte wasn't hearing her. She shoved inside the door and stalked toward Lucky, who, Jacey noticed, was staring at the woman with a lethal anger on his expression.

"*Non,* this has nothin' to do with you. If you're smart, you'll leave before you do somethin' you'll regret."

Charlotte gave a high wild laugh, never taking her eyes off him. "*I* should leave? You think I'll stand idly by while you seduce my daughter? You son of a bitch." Her eyes glittered with hatred. "The worst mistake of my life was bringing scum like you into her life. You've been nothing but a curse since I hired you."

Trepidation welled, a sudden violent surge that was tinged with panic. "What are you talking about, Mother? You didn't hire him. I did."

Charlotte looked at her, an arrested expression on her

face. Jacey turned to look at Lucky. A blank mask had dropped over his features. Her stomach clutched. "I think someone needs to explain."

"I did it for your own good, Jacinda." Her mother took one step toward her, stopped when Jacey backed away. "I couldn't allow you to get hurt with this ridiculous occupation you'd chosen. I had to do something that would bring you to your senses, show you the kind of danger that awaited you."

Jacey shook her head uncomprehendingly. "But how would you ever...how did you..."

"My cook Luella is some sort of relative of his. When asked for the name of someone who could use money and wasn't all that fussy about how he earned it, she put me in touch with Boucher."

It was as if the words had no meaning. Disjointed fragments whizzed through her head, then settled into place and began making a sort of ominous sense. She turned to Lucky, wanting, hoping for him to refute her mother's words. "I don't understand."

But his mouth flattened and he looked away, a muscle jumping in his cheek. And in that moment, an awful sense of betrayal began to well, sharp as a sword. "What were you supposed to do? Sabotage the company? Drive away what little business I had?"

"He assured me he could do both, and whatever else was needed within three months. But his word is no better than his morals. That's the kind of man you crawled into bed with, Jacinda."

Fury whipped through her, at both of them, and at the situation. Wheeling on her mother, she said, "So what does that make you, Mother? Let's talk about *your* morals. What kind of parent sets out to wreck her daughter's career, just because it doesn't happen to be one she approves of?"

"Whatever I did, I did out of love. You can't deny that, Jacinda, however much you want to. But what motivated Boucher? He's just a lowlife who'll do anything for money."

Jacey's gaze seared through Charlotte. "And you're a pathetic controlling shrew who thinks money solves everything. He was a stranger. You're my mother. There's no excuse for what you did. And the fact that you'd even try lets me know that you really don't regret your actions at all. You just regret that they didn't work."

Her mother's lips pursed. "Once you think this through—"

"—I'll still feel the same way." There was a bone-deep weariness coursing through her now, as if the weight of every one of their arguments had combined to all but bury her. "You need to leave."

Charlotte sent a look at Lucky, who was still standing motionless, watching them. Stepping closer to Jacey, she lowered her voice. "I know you're angry. But surely now you can see that this situation between the two of you is completely inappropriate."

Jacey went to the door, pulled it open. "Leave now."

For the first time, she saw a trace of uncertainty on Charlotte's face. At that moment she looked every one of her sixty years. She hesitated, then slowly walked out the door.

Without a backward glance, Jacey swung it closed behind her. But the simple act of turning to face Lucky was excruciatingly difficult. Because she despised cow-

ards, because she refused to be one, she forced herself
to meet his gaze. "Is it true?"

He watched her soberly, steadily. Silently.

She wondered if he could read how badly she wanted
a response. One that would make sense and excuse his
part in this betrayal. But the longer he remained quiet,
the more certain she was that nothing he could say could
make a dent in the brilliant pain that was slashing her
heart to ribbons. Her words were measured. "Is...
it...true?"

His dark gaze was fathomless, his expression remote. *"Oui."*

There was a quick jagged bite of agony, leaving a
path of white-hot pain in its wake. With that single
word, her world rented. Somehow she managed a jerky
nod. "Get your things." It was too difficult to continue
looking at him, so she started toward the kitchen, wanting only to get away before her emotions rose up and
swamped her.

"Ange..."

The simple endearment, threaded with desperation,
shredded what little pride she had left. Whirling, she
nearly shouted at him. "Don't! Don't think there's anything you can say that will change things. I expect this
from my mother, don't you see? I'm angry with her, furious, but what she did is so in character, it's hardly sur-
prising. But from you..." The words strangled in her
throat. She had to stop and haul in a breath, force herself to continue. "From you it's the worst kind of betrayal. You I trusted." She watched the blankness come
down over his features and wondered bitterly if it hid
his emotions, or revealed the fact that he wasn't capa-

ble of any. "You had three years to explain and now it's too late."

"T'es bien." The bleakness of his tone reflected the gray emptiness yawning inside her. One fist rhythmically clenched and released at his side. "You can kick me out of your life, your bed. That's your right. But I'm not leavin' 'til this assignment is over. Nothin' you can say will convince me to."

She jerked her shoulder as if it didn't matter. And in reality it didn't. Whether he walked away now or later, the end result was the same. Whenever it happened, she'd still be left with a yawning hole in her life and absolutely no idea of how to fill it.

Chapter 13

Jacey stared sightlessly at the research she'd compiled on Amanda Garvey. Although a few of the personal details of the woman's life left something to be desired, she'd not yet found anything that would automatically eliminate her from consideration as J. Walter's heir. Given the condition of the rest of the man's family, the possibility should have cheered her. But it would take far far more these days to raise her spirits.

Really, how fair was it to judge the woman by her unfortunate choice of men? Using the same yardstick, she herself would measure no better. Her last two lovers had been, by turn, a passionless cheat and a heartless liar. She was hardly a model for good judgment.

Seventy-two hours had passed since her life had been turned upside down. Watching Lucky walk out her door had been symbolic. He'd appeared without warning in her life. She had no doubt that when this was over he'd vanish just as abruptly. The agonizing pain that followed the certainty was becoming all too familiar.

She drew herself in, tried to focus. But a sound at her door distracted her again and she glanced up, only to freeze. As if he'd been transplanted from her thoughts, Lucky stood in her doorway, soberly watching her.

"Has Tomsino called again?"

She nodded and strove to match his tone for normalcy. The man had called her daily, pressuring her for copies of the reports she'd prepared for J. Walter. This morning she'd agreed to messenger a set of two DVDs to him, one an ostensibly sanitized version she had supposedly prepared for Garvey, and the other a carefully spliced original, minus the incriminating material they'd been putting together on Mark Garvey. She'd spent the better part of the last couple of days working on them. "I haven't heard from him since I sent them over. I hope they're enough to satisfy him for a while."

"They should convince him you're doing as he demanded. He's got far more serious things to focus on right now, anyway."

Interest stirred. "You mean your strategy is working?"

"Last night a couple of his couriers were hit for a cool quarter million. Probably drug money he was gettin' ready for launderin'. But I imagine he's feelin' the heat, especially since it's the third loss he's taken in as many days."

"Good." Her satisfaction reflected that which she heard in his voice. "I hope he's left with nothing before this is all through."

"It means things are goin' accordin' to plan. But with every loss he's goin' to get more desperate. And a desperate man gets more dangerous. Whatever happens, I don't want you alone with him."

"I don't intend to be." That was exactly why she'd messengered the DVDs to a location he'd agreed upon, rather than meeting with him. She didn't need to be reminded what the man was capable of.

"What have you discovered on the two women Mark Garvey's been photographed with?"

She shook her head. "Nothing of interest has shown up." Mark had seen two different women in four days, but the nights he'd gone to the Golden Goose and Festiva's he'd gone alone and had left the same way, early in the morning.

"Once I made sure Tomsino was otherwise occupied, I spent the last couple of evenings at the Golden Goose, talkin' to the help." His tone was businesslike, with none of the teasing warmth that had once laced it. "One waitress has worked there a couple of years. She was careful, but she did mention that it was the best-paying job she's had in a long time. She said she worked special parties after hours every couple of weeks, and makes more money that one night than she used to make in a week at her old job."

It was difficult to focus on his words when her mind insisted on torturing her with mental flashes of just how he might have elicited that information. While she'd been spending her nights talking with the surveillance teams and manning the laptop, he'd probably been charming the woman. It was no use reminding herself that jealousy was ridiculous at this point. Emotion couldn't be dictated by logic.

To distract herself, she changed the subject. "It's not

on the news yet, but they arrested Stephen Garvey this morning. My contact tells me they've charged him with twenty counts of insider trading. Something's sure to stick."

He gave a slow nod. "Now it's time to get things wrapped up on Mark Garvey, as well."

She rubbed the muscle in her shoulder that had tightened as she'd worked. "So we know the Round Table meets every other night and last night Mark had a date. Tonight could be another gambling night, but we're not doing much more than getting pictures of him in various night spots after hours. What do we do with this?"

"Us? Nothing. Except continue to turn up the heat for Tomsino. You were askin' earlier about callin' in law enforcement. It's time to bring in Vice."

His words brought both relief and a pang of desolation. Each day her nerves grew increasingly frayed. Lack of sleep added to the stress. But the end of this assignment was another sort of end between her and Lucky, as well. One even more final.

Looking away, she swallowed hard. "Good. That's good." The remaining time on this case could probably be measured in hours. Hours until they put an end to Tomsino's threats once and for all.

And hours until Lucky walked out of her life for good.

It was another two days before Lucky received word that the New Orleans Vice Squad was ready to move on the information they'd provided. On the night they decided to act, Lucky and Jacey joined one of the surveillance teams.

Jacey sat in front with Jill, the female agent, with the

computer on her lap. Lucky and Bert, the other operative, were in the back with the cameras and binoculars ready.

They'd tracked Mark Garvey to Chauncey's, an upscale strip club, at about eleven o'clock. Once they were in place, Lucky made a call to Detective Grant and they settled in to wait.

Another team was stationed in front, and they kept in constant contact via cell phones.

"I've got a positive ID on Garvey heading inside," Lucky said, lowering the binoculars. "Did you see the guy with him?"

Bert patted his camera. "Got a good shot, but didn't recognize him."

"Let's download it and have a look."

Jacey took the chip they handed her and proceeded to load it on her computer. When the picture unfolded, she felt a kick of recognition, but couldn't place the man.

"He looks familiar." She held up the computer so Lucky could lean forward and look at the screen.

"He should. It's Amanda Garvey's second husband."

"Do you think he's the one who introduced Mark Garvey to Tomsino?"

"It could have been the other way around. Whoever was to blame, they're both goin' to get caught in the net tonight."

They continued to snap pictures of the men and two women who parked in the lot behind Chauncey's and hurried inside. But when newcomers stopped arriving, the next half hour dragged.

Jacey rubbed her eyes with the heels of her hands. She didn't know what was worse; staring at the laptop or out into the darkness where shadows melded into shadows. She glanced at the clock on the dash. Time seemed to have stopped.

Abruptly the night exploded into action. A swarm of armed officers clad in dark jackets emblazoned "Vice" burst out of the darkness to race silently to the building. The door was rammed open and the officers streamed inside.

"Do you think Tomsino is in there?" She hadn't seen him enter, but he could have arrived before they did.

"Hard to imagine him not bein' there when that much money is gettin' tossed around. He's got to be around somewhere."

They waited twenty minutes, and the door opened again. This time officers were leading people outside in handcuffs. "Want me to film this?" Bert asked, the camera already in his hand.

"Definitely." Jacey put out her hand for the Steiners Lucky was using. Reluctantly he put the high-powered binoculars in her palm. She watched the surprisingly well-organized scene in silence for several minutes. Finally giving up, she gave the binoculars back to him. "I don't see Tomsino."

"He could be inside. We may as well go. I'll call Grant later and find out if they picked him up yet."

"Did you have the forensic accountant look into ownership of this property?"

"He has it in the name of a dead man."

Jacey swiveled her head to look over the seat at him. Even Bert and Jill stopped their quiet conversation to look at him.

"The deed is in his grandfather's name. A wonderful tribute," he noted caustically, "except the old man was dead twelve years before Tomsino bought the place. I turned over everything our accountant uncovered about ownership of these places to Grant."

"So they'll be looking to bring him in for questioning soon. That's good enough for now." And she might have to be satisfied with that much. Life didn't always tie up with nice neat little bows. But with the raids on his operation and the interest this sting tonight was going to generate, Tomsino had more than enough to keep his mind off Jacey's investigation.

Tomsino's interest in the case should be at an end, at any rate. She wasn't sure what kind of charges Mark Garvey would face, but they'd be very public. Given his name and reputation, they'd be given a lot of media attention. There was no way J. Walter would consider him for managing the corporation even if Jacey did recommend it.

"You can stay and find out what you can about Tomsino," she told Lucky. "I'm heading home."

"Want us to drop you off?" Jill asked.

Jacey shook her head. "I'll catch a ride with the team we have out front. I'll call you tomorrow." She shut down the computer and closed it. "With Garvey in jail for the time being, we can all get some sleep."

She could feel Lucky's dark gaze on her, but refused to look his way. The time when she'd never see him again was approaching at warp speed. So she should try getting used to this feeling of desolation. It was going to be with her for some time.

But the thought of home failed to beckon as it usually did. Instead of going straight there, she'd had the operatives drop her off at her office, so she could put the laptop away and burn the downloaded pictures on to a DVD. Placing both in the safe, she'd carefully relocked it and then, oddly reluctant, drove the rental car home.

She knew the cause of this aversion, of course. The sense of serenity her house had once held was gone. There were too many memories just lurking around the corner of each room, on the stairway, the hallway. She was hopelessly certain it would be a very long time before she stopped looking up unexpectedly and seeing Lucky everywhere.

Entering the house, she locked the door behind her and headed up the stairs, already considering the benefits of a long hot bath. It might relax her before settling into bed.

But on the heels of that thought came the recollection of lying with Lucky in that same tub, sharing wine and finger food by candlelight. With a mental curse, she turned toward her bedroom instead, even while recognizing it would be haunted by similar memories.

In the act of reaching for the light switch, she froze, something deep in her unconscious screaming a warning. But before she could back away, she heard the distinctive sound of a gun being cocked.

"Glad you could join me, Ms. Wheeler. I've been waiting for you."

She didn't need the light to identify the owner of the voice. Vinny Tomsino. She flipped it on anyway, saw him sitting in an easy chair next to the window. He would have been looking out of it, waiting for her arrival. And she'd walked straight into his arms.

A cold shudder snaked down her spine. The NOPD

was probably combing the city for him at this very moment. No one would expect to find him here.

"What do you want?" She didn't bother trying to make her words sound more welcoming.

"That's a very interesting question." He was studying her with more than a hint of malevolence in his gaze. "I thought I was quite clear about that in our conversations earlier. But I've been getting very little of what I want for several days now."

How much did he know? What could she afford to tell him? The questions circled frantically in her head, but the answers eluded her. Cautiously, she said, "I don't know what you mean. I did exactly as you requested."

"That doesn't do me much good now." His face was twisted in an ugly mask. "My plans have fallen apart and I need to get out of town quickly. Since my personal finances have taken a turn for the worse, lately, I figured you'd be willing to help. I understand you can well afford it."

"You want me to write you a check to leave town?"

"To leave the country, actually." He undid the button on his suit coat and shifted to a more comfortable position. "Just until interest in me dies down around here. A couple of hundred thousand should do it."

She said the first thing that came into her head. "The banks don't open until nine tomorrow."

"Which is one of the reasons I'm going to keep you company tonight."

She fought the dread that threatened to bury her and honed in on his words. "One of the reasons."

He gave her a small smile, showing uneven teeth. "We'll wait for your lover together. He and I have some unfinished business. I'm afraid I suspect that he might have had something to do with my recent reversal of fortunes. When do you expect him?"

"I don't," she said bluntly, and only too honestly. "We're no longer seeing each other."

He gave a laugh. "Figured he wouldn't stick around long. But you can get him here." He gestured with the gun barrel. "Where's your cell phone? Call him up. It'd be a shame to have this party and not invite him."

Lucky waited for Detective Grant to finish supervising the arrests before approaching him. The man was speaking on the phone to what sounded like his superior, when he looked up and saw Lucky. He held up a hand to gesture for him to wait, then spoke for another few seconds.

Disconnecting, he nodded in Lucky's direction. "Thanks for the tip. We picked up nearly half a million in cash inside."

Lucky whistled. "Any sign of Tomsino?"

The man shook his head. "And no one has admitted to seeing him there this evening. But it's only a matter of time until we pick him up. I hear he's having all sorts of bad luck this week. Got a turf war starting up, with raids on his operations. Must be costing him a bundle."

"Is that so?" Lucky's voice was bland.

The detective stared hard at him. "But you wouldn't know anything about that?"

"Can't say that I do." Lucky shoved his hands in his pockets and rocked back on his heels. "What type of gamblin' activity was he runnin', anyway?"

Grant looked back at the building. "He had himself

a real sweet deal. Collected a bunch of high rollers and gave them a place to have their games. Worked himself into becoming their bankroll when they ran out of cash. Some of those guys we took out of here are into him for some serious money."

The man continued talking, but Lucky's mind was elsewhere. If Tomsino was on the run from the cops, where would he go? Not to any of his homes. He wouldn't dare. And who would he trust at a time when his businesses were being raided? He'd have to realize that the information leading to the successful attacks had come from someone in his organization. So that meant he couldn't trust any of his colleagues. Hotels would be too risky. So where was he?

Nerves twisted through him. He'd feel better if Jacey had stayed here with him until he could see her safely home. Not that she would welcome his company, but at least his mind would be relieved…

A horrible thought struck him. He spun on his heel and sprinted away, leaving the detective in midsentence.

"Hey! Where you going?"

Tossing the words over his shoulder, he yelled, "I think I know where Tomsino might have gone."

The light in Jacey's bedroom was on. Was she awake then, maybe working on business? Or did she have an unwelcome guest? He let himself into the gated court- yard, and slipped behind some mimosa trees to get a bet- ter visual angle into the bedroom. The terrace doors off the bedroom were closed. Each night he'd been in bed they'd been opened. He wasn't sure if the fact was rel- evant or not.

He looked up and down the street. There was little traffic at this hour. Which meant, he thought grimly, heading to the side of the home, there'd be no witnesses to his breaking and entering.

Jacey's home featured two balconies one on top of the other. The one on the bottom floor led to the living room. Upstairs was her bedroom. He scrambled up on the lacy wrought-iron railing and balanced his weight on the balls of his feet. Tensing, he sprang upward, his arms outstretched.

Catching the lower rungs of the upstairs balcony in his hands, he laboriously pulled himself up, his upper body shuddering with the strain. In all likelihood Jacey had just been so tired she'd fallen asleep without bothering to shut the light off. As he worked a leg up to the balcony, he tried to make himself believe it. And if that was true all that would have happened was that he would have gotten a workout.

Once he landed on the upstairs balcony, he tried to find a position where he could peer in through a crack afforded by the sheers at the window. By lying on his back, his head cocked to an uncomfortable angle, he could see the bed. It was empty. But he heard voices inside, and strained to listen. He recognized Jacey's and struggled to make out the other, deeper voice.

But in the next moment he heard a low harsh laugh that was all too familiar.

Vinny Tomsino.

An icy river coursed through his chest. His mind searched frantically for a way to get Jacey out of there safely. His gaze lingering on the doors, he crouched down and moved to the edge of the balcony. Climbing up on the railing again, he jumped lightly up to catch the edge of the roof.

Either it was damp, or his palms were sweaty. His grip slipped, and he nearly fell, his legs kicking as he dangled there, his hands grappling for a firmer purchase. Tightening his grasp, he pulled himself upward, inch by excruciating inch, his feet walking up the side of the house until he could pull himself up and over.

He took a few moments to lie there panting, before digging in his pockets and taking out a handful of coins. He positioned himself directly above the door, and crouched there. Then he slipped the knife from his sheath and held it ready.

A penny was dropped, but it fell well away from the windows and rolled harmlessly across the balcony and over the edge. Lucky tried another, this time managing to make a clink on the glass panes. He stilled, held his breath, but nothing happened. Again he threw a coin, heard the slight sound it made as it landed.

There was a noise at the door below. Someone was unlocking it. He drew back a little until he could be sure of who was coming out on the balcony.

He saw the gun first, followed by an arm encased in a shirtsleeve. He forced himself to wait until he saw the top of Tomsino's balding pate as he edged warily out to investigate. When the man was directly beneath him, Lucky launched himself through the air.

Something must have warned the other man. He turned his head, saw the form coming toward him, and began to swing the gun in his direction when Lucky's weight hit him, knocking Tomsino to the ground.

He'd brought the knife up as he landed, aiming for

the man's neck, but his own momentum carried him farther, faster, than he'd expected. The two of them went down, weapons flying, as they engaged in a silent deadly battle.

Lucky landed a kick to the man's ribs, heard the breath wheeze out of Tomsino, but his struggles didn't weaken. Tomsino sent a fist to Lucky's jaw that he only managed to half duck. It caught him in the temple and red dots danced across his vision. He caught the man around the neck and used both thumbs on his Adam's apple. Done correctly the move could crush a person's larynx.

They rolled across the small area, each struggling for the upper hand. Vinny tried to use his extra weight to his advantage, attempting to pin Lucky down before swinging at him. Lucky ducked and the man's fist crashed into the cement.

"Don't move."

Both of them froze when they heard the words, saw Tomsino's gun clutched in Jacey's steady hands inches away from Tomsino's temple. "You don't know how much I want you to give me a reason to use this. I would. Willingly."

"You're making a mistake," Tomsino said venomously.

Lucky felt an odd sense of pride as he watched Jacey handle the Glock expertly. Tomsino let go of him, he picked himself up, and sent his fist into the man's nose. "*Non,* it is you who made the mistake."

Detective Grant had been called, the police had come and gone, and it was nearing dawn. Lucky shut the door on the last officer and looked at Jacey. He wasn't sure he liked what he saw. She looked as though one strong breeze would blow her away. He wanted to gather her close, to celebrate their survival in the most primitive, primal way possible.

He folded his arms across his chest to keep from reaching for her. Only a few short days ago he would have had that right. Now she wouldn't even look at him.

"Detective Grant said Mark started talkin' immediately when they took him in, hopin' to get the charges reduced." Discussing the case gave him an excuse to linger, when he was certain she wanted him to follow the cops out her door. He couldn't quite bring himself to do that. Not yet. "Seems like he's racked up a gamblin' debt of close to a million dollars." He couldn't imagine having that much money, much less tossing it away on the draw of the cards. There was something pretty warped about someone who'd do so.

"Tomsino kept lettin' the debt run up to get him well and truly hooked. Then he started strong-armin' him. Had him doin' some legal work on the side for him, mostly advice on how to hide his activities. But I'll bet the whole time he was thinkin' of a way to get his fingers on Garvey Enterprises. A shippin' business would be mighty handy for someone with Tomsino's sidelines."

"So how did they? Find out, I mean?" Curiosity might be rousing her from her earlier shock. She was still slumped against the wall, arms wrapped around her waist, but her voice seemed stronger.

"Garvey said they had someone inside J. Walter's bank who tipped them off about the money transfer when he hired you. And Jeffrey isn't working the low-level position in the mail room for no reason."

"He intercepted the contract."

Lucky almost smiled. She was always quick to put the pieces together. "He opens and scans all of Grandpa's mail, or at least what he can get his hands on. He turned the information over to Mark, Mark passed it on to Tomsino. Hard to tell who connected the dots to figure out what you were investigatin'."

"It was probably a group effort. One of them discovered the information about J. Walter's health, and that, coupled with the transfer and contract was enough for them to start drawing some conclusions."

"The fact that Lianna came to you makes it pretty obvious that she was in on these details, too."

"If Jeffrey is aligned against J. Walter with Mark, he's probably the one who told her. But I doubt she knew anything about Tomsino's plans. He would never have allowed her to approach you. Most likely she was just tryin' to obtain information that would get her kid in position to inherit."

"Poor J. Walter." Real pity was evident in her tone. "Family isn't always a blessing. His is more of a curse."

If ever there were an opening, he knew this was it. And it might be the only one he was going to get. Nerves jumped in his belly. "Blood can't guarantee understanding, or even love. You know that as well as I do."

She stiffened, and he could almost see the ice shooting into her veins. With a feeling of despair, he wondered if there was anything he could do, anything he could say to melt it. "I met my *maman* exactly three times in my life, when she'd get desperate enough to come back home and try to talk my *grand-mère* into givin' her money. Even when I was a kid I knew she had less feelin' for me than a dog did for her whelps. We can't pick our families. I wonder how well we'd do if we could."

Her smile was tight. "I'm guessing I'd be a washout. Because we *can* pick our friends." She paused for an emotion-filled moment. "And under the circumstances, I can't claim to have been too successful."

She blinked back tears and a vise squeezed in his chest. He was a fool to stand here, as if he could try and reason away something that couldn't be forgiven. In the end, he neither gave an excuse nor begged forgiveness. But he could offer what was in his heart. Accept or deny it, she would be given that much choice.

"You asked me once about the turnin' point in my life. I couldn't answer your question then. I still can't. Life is a series of decisions. Some we make consciously, the others are dictated by some instinct we don't even understand." He stopped, realization slamming in to him with the force of a Mack truck.

Slowly, still finding his way, he continued. "I met with your mother and I took her money." The fact that he'd eventually returned it didn't change his original intent. "I went to your office that first day to put you out of business." He'd never doubted his success, and his actions had been easy to justify. Her mother's reasons had been valid. Hers *was* a dangerous business. She *had* been out of her league. And she *hadn't* belonged there. That was what he'd thought.

He'd been wrong.

"There just isn't always somethin' you can point to and say, that's it. That's where it all changed." At least there hadn't been for him. "After you hired me I floated along from one day to the next, from one week to the next, and still I told myself I was goin' to follow through with it. I had half a dozen different plans for makin' you miserable, or scared or just broke. And every mornin' I'd walk in and see your face, and find another reason to wait a bit longer."

Her eyes cut to his. And as usual, the hint of vulnerability he saw in them cut him off at the knees. "I can't say that it was friendship that stopped me, because we weren't friends. Not yet. And I can't point to a single moment when I made the decision not to follow through, because there wasn't one. All I know is one day I accepted the fact that I wasn't going to. I didn't decide not to, I just realized I wasn't." That distinction was important, although he couldn't have explained why. "It wasn't because I could use the position to better myself. Tomsino paid far better for less. Or because I thought I could seduce you into givin' me more. Your proposition scared me to death."

"I know." Her words were full of tears, tears he knew she'd never shed in front of him. She swallowed hard before going on. "Why did it? You had dozens of women."

"I never had anythin' to lose with any of them. But you and I had grown close in a way I'd never expected." Had never experienced. It still had the power to stagger him, the relationship that had developed between the ex-debutante and the Cajun with bayou blood beating in his veins. It had been the last thing he'd expected.

"I have no idea how or why we ever became friends. But when we did, I didn't want to risk that. Not for anythin'. So I'm not goin' to stand here and say I wanted to

tell you the truth a thousand times." The words would
have been easy, but there wasn't a shred of honesty in
them. He jammed his hands in his pockets. "If I'd had my
way, you would never have found out what brought me
to you that day. We wouldn't be havin' this conversation."

Something was curling through the weight of futil-
ity Jacey had carried for the last several days. Something
that felt suspiciously like hope. "What was it you didn't
want to risk?"

"You." He shook his head, as if attempting to clear
it. "Us. I was willin' to settle for less than I wanted, because it was more than I had ever expected."

Shock stunned her, robbed her of the careful guard
she'd affected. "You...wanted...me?"

"The first time I saw you I forgot to breathe." His
voice was a murmur, and there was a faraway look to
his eyes. "You were wearin' one of those killer suits with
the prissy shirts even then. You were wary of me at first.
You had good instincts. And you argued with me over
the case file on your desk."

Her throat full, she cleared it. "I remember." Her
stomach had hollowed out, as if she was riding a roller
coaster, all sharp turns and steep drops.

His gaze suddenly cleared and was sharp enough to
see all the way through her. "A better man would accept
how far apart we are, in background, experiences. Your
mother is right about that. Me, I'm a selfish sort. I only
care 'bout how we are together."

He crossed to her then, quick deliberate strides and
braced his hands on the wall on either side of her, ef-
fectively caging her. "When I'm with you nothin' else
matters. Not where we came from. Not who or what we

are. *Je t'aime,* Jacey. I love you. If you can learn to trust me again, we can be lovers, if that's what you want." He leaned in closer, so just a breath of air separated their bodies. "Or if you want to be only friends, that's how it will be."

Emotions zinged through her, bright whirling dervishes that threatened to implode in one brilliant rainbow. An image of her mother flashed into her mind and she recognized the choice she was faced with. She could send Lucky away, and take a step closer to the life Charlotte would choose for her. Or she could stand firm and reach for what she really wanted.

"I thought you said you didn't want to be friends anymore." As she spoke, she smoothed her hands up over his chest, linking them around his neck.

His smile was slow and devastating, but it was the tinge of relief in it that quieted her jittery nerves once and for all. "I want," he murmured against her throat, as his mouth brushed over the pulse at its base, "whatever you will give me."

She tilted her head back to look into his eyes, all teasing abruptly gone. "I love you, Lucky. I'll offer you that. And I'll give you babies if you want them, too, and a life together. As a matter of fact, I'll give you as much as you're willing to take."

His eyes, those dark, wicked eyes, held promises in their depths. "I'm a very greedy man, *cher.* I'll take it all."

Epilogue

Six months later

Rain drizzled desultorily through the patches of fog, further dampening the spirits of all the mourners crowding the graveyard. White monuments lined the narrow walkways, making it impossible to draw close enough to hear the final prayers before J. Walter Garvey was put to rest in his family vault.

Jacey was content to linger near the gate at the entrance. The umbrella in Lucky's hand kept them relatively dry, but still she was reminded of the night she'd agreed to take J. Walter's case. It was as if the intervening months had brought them full circle.

She wasn't certain which of the man's heirs had made the funeral arrangements, but somehow she thought he would have disapproved of the entire process. He hadn't been one to enjoy crowds or pageantry, and his funeral had included both. The church had been overflowing, a tribute to his standing in the community, and each of his family members had been present in the processional.

As if plucking the thought from her head, Lucky murmured, "So just when are Stephen and Mark Garvey's trials scheduled for? Have you heard?"

"I think Stephen's is early next year. Mark's lawyer will probably file for one continuance after another, until he gets the best deal possible."

A couple trying to edge through the crowd jostled them, and Lucky slipped his arm around Jacey's waist to bring her closer to him. "I don't think he has much left to offer. He gave up his cousin, Wharton, to Detective Grant almost immediately."

She remembered. According to Mark Garvey, Tomsino had been Jeffrey Wharton's drug connection while he was on campus, and their association had continued when Wharton had returned to New Orleans. The NOPD had already been building a case against the kid when that news had surfaced. It was probably only a matter of time until an arrest warrant was issued for him, as well.

A feeling of sadness lanced through her. J. Walter had deserved better than that from his family. She'd heard that Rupert was on the verge of losing the small fortune he'd recently invested in his girlfriend's thoroughbred operation, so apparently the older man's opinion of his son's spendthrift ways had been on target.

"The one I feel sorry for is Amanda." She leaned her head against Lucky's black-clad shoulder for a moment. "Nothing in our investigation suggested that she wouldn't be capable of stepping in and learning the business. But J. Walter wouldn't even consider her." Her marital merry-go-round had damned her in the older man's eyes, perhaps unfairly. His final will wouldn't have been revealed to the family yet, but Jacey knew he'd left operation of the company to the board of directors.

"You did the job you were hired for, gatherin' the information he requested. The final decision was his to make."

She knew that, of course. But she doubted she'd ever grow as adept as Lucky at separating her emotions from the outcome of a case.

Tilting her head up to his, she demanded, "And that's it? You never have concerns about the way things turned out? What about the arrangement you set in place with those two men who split up Tomsino's operation?"

He shrugged. "I gave Grant everythin' I had. It's the NOPD's concern, now. At least we can be grateful Tomsino will be put away for a lengthy time."

That was true enough. It hadn't taken the police long to get warrants to search all his businesses, even— thanks to Lucky—the ones not in his name. The records they'd found had provided them with enough damaging evidence to put him away for good. Since he'd already proved he was a flight risk, he was languishing in jail until his trial, despite the protests of his high-priced defense attorney.

The crowd seemed to be drifting toward them, indicating the ceremony was at an end. They turned and began to make their way out of the cemetery. Lucky handed her the umbrella while he dug into his pants pocket for the keys. On the surface, he did a fair job of blending in with the other dark-garbed mourners, in his black jacket and pants. He was growing increasingly adept at maneuvering his way around in what he referred to as high society. His easy charm almost completely hid the hints of danger acquired from life on mean streets and backwoods bayous. She found herself hoping that he never completely lost those rough edges. They were a part of the man she'd fallen in love with, and as such, precious to her.

He caught her eye on him then and started to smile, until the expression on her face stopped him. "Regrets?"

Jacey shook her head, reached for his hand and locked their fingers. The diamond on her finger glittered even in the fog. "Not anymore. Let's skip the funeral dinner. I'd rather finalize wedding plans."

Bringing her hand to his lips, he pressed a kiss to it. "If I'd had my way, it would have happened six months ago."

She laughed at his disgruntled tone. "Your *grand-mère* wants a proper Cajun wedding, and the preparations take time."

A frown flickered on his brow. "But is that what *you* want?"

She thought again of the customs his grandmother had patiently explained to her, each one steeped in the culture and tradition of his heritage. "Very much." For her, their wedding would symbolize more than their union; it would meld their worlds so that backgrounds— experiences—no longer mattered. All that would matter was the life they built together.

"I'm looking forward to all the traditions. The charm pulls in the cake, jumping over the broom with you and even the charivari, although I'm not quite sure what that entails."

His thumb brushed over her knuckles and the look in
his eyes was heated. "Don't be wastin' your energies on
some silly customs, *cher*. Save them for the honeymoon."

Because her knees were going weak, she straightened
them. "Maybe you're the one who should be…" The
rest of the sentence was forgotten as she caught sight of
Peter Brummond ahead of them, getting into a chauf-
feured car.

Lucky's gaze followed hers. "I heard there's some
doubt about the paternity of the child his wife is carryin'."

"What?" Her attention snapped to him. "Where did
you hear that?"

He lifted a shoulder, nudged her to get her moving
again. "At that affair you dragged me to last week.
Guess I won't have to kneecap him, after all. He's already got plenty of trouble in his paradise."

A better person wouldn't have felt a niggling sense
of satisfaction at the news. Jacey decided she could live
with the fact that she was no saint. "He isn't important
to us."

"*Non,* but she is." He nodded toward the limo pulling
up behind Brummond's for the lone woman standing on
the sidewalk. Charlotte Wheeler waited impatiently for the
driver to stop, get out and come around to open her door.

Jacey's lips firmed. She hadn't returned any of her
mother's phone calls. Had had only one short conversation with her five months ago. She hadn't been naive
enough to expect an apology, but she had expected that
the woman would have had the sense not to bring up her
opinions of Lucky again. They were never going to
agree on that topic and Jacey was far happier not having to deal with her at all.

"Have you sent her an invitation?" Lucky murmured.

"They haven't been sent yet," she hedged.

They both watched as the woman was handed into the car and the door closed. Moments later, the driver rounded the limo, got inside and the car pulled away from the curb.

"My *grand-mère* won't live forever." With a slight tug on her hand, they began to move again, in the direction of the Firebird. "Your mother is goin' to be the only grandparent our children will have."

Thoughts of having Lucky's children sent a warm glow spreading through her stomach, but she still muttered, "Then God help them."

He regarded her soberly. "Family is important, darlin'. Neither of us have enough to be careless with it. You'll be happier in the long run if you patch things up with your mother."

"How can you even want that? She has nothing but loathing for you. She's never going to stop trying to cause trouble between us."

He pursed his lips, as if considering her words. "I figure I've got the best revenge. Me bein' married to you will drive her crazy for the rest of her life. I can afford to be generous." He tugged on her hand to bring her into his arms. Uncaring of the curious eyes around them, she went willingly. "She can't hurt us, unless we let her," he murmured, his lips close to her ear. He dropped one quick stinging kiss beneath the lobe, making her shiver. "And we're not goin' to let her, are we?"

His words made sense, even as she realized he was underestimating the problem. Her mother would never change her meddlesome ways, but their effect on Jacey would be minimized. In the face of their happiness, Lucky was right. They could afford to be generous.

"All right. I'll put her on the guest list as soon as we get home."

Approval shone in his eyes, as well as a sizzling steam that never failed to turn the blood in her veins molten. "It can wait a while longer," he drawled, his tone rife with promise. He brushed a kiss over her lips, returned to linger. "First I think we need to start practicin' for that honeymoon."

* * * * *

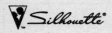

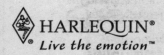

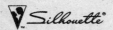

INTIMATE MOMENTS™

and award-winning author
VIRGINIA KANTRA
present
STOLEN MEMORY
(IM #1347)

The next book in her exciting miniseries

TROUBLE IN EDEN

**Small town, big secrets—
and hearts on the line!**

Dedicated cop Laura Baker is used to having all the answers. But when reclusive inventor Simon Ford wakes up on the floor of his lab with a case of amnesia and a missing fortune in rubies, all Laura has are questions. As her investigation heats up, so does her attraction to the aloof millionaire. Can she find the missing jewels…before she loses her heart?

*Available February 2005
at your favorite retail outlet.*

And look for the other electrifying titles in the TROUBLE IN EDEN miniseries available from Silhouette Intimate Moments:
**All a Man Can Do (IM #1180), All a Man Can Ask (IM #1197),
All a Man Can Be (IM #1215)**

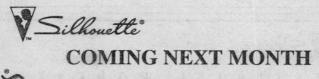

COMING NEXT MONTH